THE BUTT OF T

FIRST BULL Run was the first real battle of the war. But the reason it's embarrassing is that's where my great-great-great-great-uncle Cyrus Hinkleman was wounded.

Did a cannonball blast off Uncle Cyrus's leg as he bravely charged over the field? Was he stabbed by a bayonet while trying to capture a flag, which for some reason was really important back then? Was he shot as he leaped over a fence and into the enemy lines?

Oh no. He was shot in the butt.

That's right, he got the bum rush, the stuck butt, the flank attack, the sheared rear. Which can only mean one thing. He was running away when he was shot. No brave charge for Uncle Cyrus. He turned chicken and fled.

At the hospital, his butt wound got infected. For a lot of soldiers in the war, an infection meant amputation. A bullet in the knee could lead to the doctor cutting off your leg so that the infection wouldn't spread to the rest of your body.

But how do you amputate a butt?

So Uncle Cyrus lay on his stomach in a hospital bed for a couple of weeks until the infection killed him. This was my family's great contribution to the Civil War. One bullet. One butt.

OTHER BOOKS YOU MAY ENJOY

★ STONEWALL ★
★ HINKLEMAN ★

AND THE

·BATTLE OF BULL RUN·

STONEWALL HINKLEMAN

AND THE

BATTLE OF BULL RUN

TOM ANGLEBERGER
& MICHAEL HEMPHILL

PUFFIN BOOKS
An Imprint of Penguin Group (USA)

PUFFIN BOOKS
Published by the Penguin Group
Penguin Group (USA) LLC
375 Hudson Street
New York, New York 10014

USA * Canada * UK * Ireland * Australia
New Zealand * India * South Africa * China

penguin.com
A Penguin Random House Company

First published in the United States of America by Dial Books for Young Readers,
a division of Penguin Young Readers Group, 2009
Published by Puffin Books, an imprint of Penguin Young Readers Group, 2014

THE LIBRARY OF CONGRESS HAS CATALOGED THE DIAL BOOKS EDITION AS FOLLOWS:
Hemphill, Michael.
Stonewall Hinkleman and the Battle of Bull Run / by Michael Hemphill and Sam Riddleburger.
p. cm.
Summary: While participating in a reenactment of the Battle of Bull Run, twelve-year-old
Stonewall Hinkleman is transported back to the actual Civil War battle by means of a magic bugle.
ISBN 978-0-8037-3179-0 (hc)
1. Bull Run, 1st Battle of, Va., 1861—Juvenile fiction.
[1. Bull Run, 1st Battle of, Va., 1861—Fiction.
2. United States—History—Civil War, 1861–1865—Fiction.
3. Time travel—Fiction.] I. Riddleburger, Sam. II. Title.
PZ7.H37747St 2009
[Fic]—dc22

Puffin Books ISBN 978-0-14-751182-9

Printed in the United States of America

1 3 5 7 9 10 8 6 4 2

This book is dedicated to Civil War buffs, historians,
scholars and re-enactors. Forgive us . . .
we couldn't control
Stonewall Hinkleman's big mouth.

Special thanks to Caryn, Liz, Nancy, Tuesday, Jasmin, Jeanine,
Julia, Cece, Naomi, Emily, Meg, Mary Ann, Wayne,
Charlie, Oscar, Babs, Madge, Cindy, Lolly, Chip, Linda,
Fun Teachers, Cool Librarians, Kind Booksellers, Kidlit Bloggers,
and Civil War Journey tour guide Robert Freis
for his expert advice on the Battle of Bull Run.

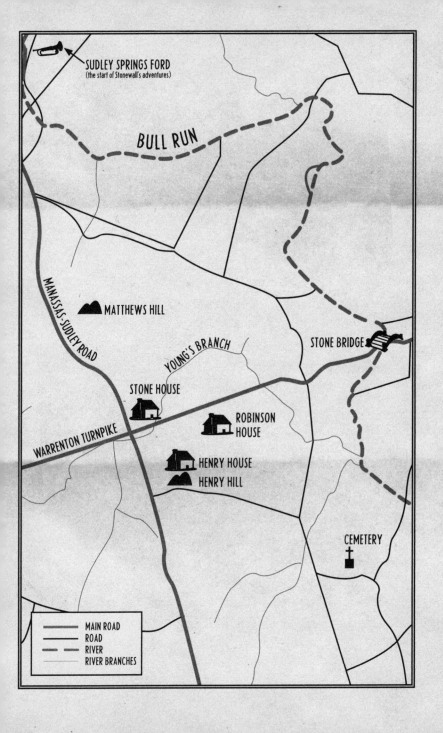

★ STONEWALL ★
HINKLEMAN

AND THE

BATTLE OF BULL RUN

CHAPTER ONE

ALL RIGHT, let's get the whole name thing out of the way quickly.

My name is Stonewall Hinkleman.

No, it's not a nickname. It's my real name. Like I tell my parents—even Stonewall Jackson's real name wasn't Stonewall. But they don't listen and it's too late now anyway. I'm stuck with it.

So, you'd think I could at least go by my middle name, right? It's Traveler, after Robert E. Lee's horse. Yeah, that's right, a horse!

I'm Stonewall Traveler Hinkleman and if you think that's as bad as it gets, you haven't heard the worst part.

You see, both of my parents are Civil War reenactors. This means my dad—who's really a geeky computer tech—dresses up in a uniform and runs around in fields with a bunch of other boring guys who are all pretending they are in the Civil War. My mother pretends she's a nurse, even though in real life she barfs at the sight of blood.

1

Going to reenactments is my life almost every weekend. I have fought, I have cried, I have argued, I have resisted, but they make me go too. I am twelve years old and I am the bugle boy, probably the dorkiest thing you can be. Even if I wanted to—and I don't—I'm not old enough to march with the troops and shoot a gun. And I'm too old to still think watching all of this is cool. So no gun, no bayonet, just stand around blowing a horn.

Dad says I should be proud that I'm the one who calls the soldiers to action.

"Someday, Stonewall," he says in his real high, nasally voice, "you'll begin to appreciate your heritage and the history of the American event that pitted brother against brother in a battle of wills over the very fate of our nation."

He runs on like that all the time. I have to listen to hours of it every weekend while we drive to one stupid reenactment after another.

"You are named after a great general, a great scholar and a great man," my father likes to say.

Whatever, Dad. Did I mention that Stonewall Jackson was shot by HIS OWN MEN?!?!

This particular weekend we're heading to the reenactment that's not only boring like all the others but personally embarrassing.

We'll be reenacting a battle called Manassas. First Manassas, that is, not Second Manassas. It's also called Bull Run, as in First Bull Run and Second Bull Run. That's how stupid all this really is. Not only are there different names for the same

2

battle, but some battles were fought in the same place twice. Get it right the first time already!

First Bull Run was the first real battle of the war. But the reason it's embarrassing is that's where my great-great-great-great-uncle Cyrus Hinkleman was wounded.

Did a cannonball blast off Uncle Cyrus's leg as he bravely charged over the field? Was he stabbed by a bayonet while trying to capture a flag, which for some reason was real important back then? Was he shot as he leaped over a fence and into the enemy lines?

Oh no. He was shot in the butt.

That's right, he got the bum rush, the stuck butt, the flank attack, the sheared rear. Which can only mean one thing. He was running away when he was shot. No brave charge for Uncle Cyrus. He turned chicken and fled.

At the hospital, his butt wound got infected. For a lot of soldiers in the war, an infection meant amputation. A bullet in the knee could lead to the doctor cutting off your leg so that the infection wouldn't spread to the rest of your body.

But how do you amputate a butt?

So Uncle Cyrus lay on his stomach in a hospital bed for a couple of weeks until the infection killed him. This was my family's great contribution to the Civil War. One bullet. One butt.

Yet, somehow it's enough to get my father misty-eyed.

As we walk across the field to where we'll pitch our tent, Dad babbles on and on about sacrifice and resolve and our family's proud heritage.

3

"Proud heritage? Dad, he got shot in the butt!"

I shouldn't have said that out loud.

The dreamy look on my father's face fades. He slings his musket to his other shoulder and tells me to shut up. My mother, wearing a white shawl over a long blue dress, gives me her I'm-very-disappointed look.

But it's true and they know it, and that's the only reason they're mad. Our proud heritage is nothing more than one scared uncle running for his life.

We never seem to reenact that.

You want to know what a reenactment is really like? It doesn't matter which battle it is, because they're all the same.

A big bunch of guys wearing blue Yankee costumes come huffing up the hill. Waiting for them are my dad's friends—a big bunch of guys in gray Confederate costumes. We jump out and we charge. I have to blow my bugle and everybody else fires their guns, which don't have ammo but are still ridiculously loud. About half of them fall down and pretend to be dead. They roll around with these hilarious grimaces on their faces. Then they're still for a while, probably taking a nap or eating a candy bar, until the "battle" moves somewhere else and they get back up and rejoin the "fight."

Whoopee! And I'll give you three good reasons why it's worse than just boring.

First, it's hot. Second, we're wearing wool outfits, because you've got to be "authentic" at reenactments and that's sup-

4

posedly what the real soldiers wore. Third, I'm missing Emagination Camp to be here. It's basically two weeks of building Lego robots, which I personally consider the best possible use of summer.

But once again, it conflicts with this stupid reenactment. And God forbid I should miss even one weekend of magic with my father and his special friends.

The really sad thing about all this is that I've also come to the realization that camp is my one and only chance of getting a girlfriend. The girls at my school have pretty much made it clear that they'd rather die than be seen talking to me. I can hardly blame them. I'm not real tall, my red hair never sits still, and my teeth stick out "six ways to Sunday," as my dentist says. (I'm getting braces before the summer's done . . . another big score for Stonewall!) And the girls have seen me at my worst—whining, being a nerd, getting pushed around, and, most recently, getting a wedgie from Cal Smallwood on the last day of school.

There *is* one really cool girl who has just starting coming to the reenactments. She's amazingly cute even in a nurse's uniform that's 150 years out of style. She's got a lot of bushy brown hair and big brown eyes, and Mom is always trying to get me to talk to her, but there's no way that's going to happen with me dressed like a dorky bugle boy.

So, camp would be a chance to start with a clean slate—no prior embarrassments and no uniform.

But, no. Once again, I'm hauling the uniform and a bunch of other fake Civil War junk about a mile from the parking lot to our campsite. We stop every two seconds because my dad sees someone he knows and has to talk to them.

Worse, since my name is so stupid, every single one of these guys remembers it.

"Hey, Stonewall!" they yell, or, "How are the troops, Stonewall?"

I fake a smile. My dad gets really mad if I "embarrass" him in front of his friends. He doesn't seem to mind that he's embarrassing me all weekend.

Okay, I admit that I *may* have once found reenactments cool . . . when I was six years old. Pitching our canvas tent in a grassy field, or on nice nights just sleeping outside under the stars. Staying up late cooking stew over a campfire. Watching my dad and his buds march off with their shiny muskets and sharp bayonets—hearing their Rebel yells and gunfire—and really being able to pretend they were soldiers in a war.

But that was before Dad turned me into a bugle boy. And before I'd seen each reenactment like five times already. Sometimes I feel like we're reenacting reenactments. And I'm starting to worry that what I'm really reenacting out here is the dorkiness of my father's life.

"I just wish I had had these opportunities at your age," he'll often say.

Which makes me think that if he's turned out the way he has while NOT going to reenactments as a kid, what chance do I have?

Sometimes when I'm complaining about my crappy life, some kid at school will say, "What's the big deal? Reenactments sound cool and it's got to be better than sitting at home all weekend."

Wrong! Sitting at home all weekend rocks compared to going to a reenactment. Think about all the things that are good in life: DVDs, TV, PlayStation, Dr Pepper, ice cream, french fries, YouTube and MySpace, Taco Bell, comfortable chairs, sleeping late, mattresses, flush toilets, Reese's Puffs cereal, Lego robots, Japanese comic books, and clothing that doesn't itch like holy heck.

None of those had been invented yet when the Civil War happened. Or even if they had you couldn't get them while fighting the Civil War. So that's why you can't have them at a reenactment.

Now, that's a great lesson to learn once. Whew, old-timey folks had it hard and we just take modern stuff for granted. Yay! Great lesson! I'm a better person now!

But like I said: You only need to do it once. They've been dragging me to these things since I was six. So that's six years times at least ten reenactments a year. That's at least sixty times I've learned the stupid lesson already!

Welcome to my luxury accommodations. I take the bedroll off my back, roll it out on the ground, and presto! Room for one at the Bull Run Hilton. Only a quarter mile to the nearest Porta-John.

At least I don't have to sleep in the tent with my parents anymore. It's an authentic historical genuine reproduction tent, which means it's totally worthless, unwaterproofed, and tiny. It's just a piece of canvas held up by three poles and

7

staked to the ground. But it does provide some cover. While they go off to chat with friends, I dive into their tent and pull out my Game Boy.

The only problem is I forget to hit MUTE first. The start-up *squelch* sends my mom running.

"Stonewall, put down that video game. You know I don't like you playing that in camp," says my mom. "Plus, those games are too violent."

Too violent? We're here reenacting a freaking war, Mom! Dad can shoot reenactors, but I can't kill orcs on my Game Boy?

Dad rushes in to back her up. "I've told you about bringing anything *farby* to our reenactments. A successful weekend is . . ."

"An authentic weekend," I say, finishing the cliché that has been my life.

Farby, in case you haven't figured it out yet, is anything "not authentic to the period." (Don't ask me where they got the word *farby* from, because I don't know or care.) I've tried pointing out before that everyone here is farby since none of us were here during "the period," but they don't listen.

Dad says, "I'm going to clean my musket now. Stonewall, why don't you come over here and polish your bugle?"

"Because I don't want to?"

"I'm not going to listen to backtalk all weekend," my mother says. "Now put that game down before I take it away."

It goes on like this, until I finally yell "All right already" loud enough for nearby campsites to hear.

This makes my mother extra-mad and, realizing that I've gone a little too far, I get up to get the bugle from my pack.

Only it's not there. I know I didn't leave it in the car. I must have left it at home.

My father goes ballistic. He doesn't want to shout at me because then I would be "embarrassing him." So there's a lot of hissing from my mother and low growling threats from my father.

"How could you have left your bugle at home?" he rumbles.

"I don't know," I say. "I'm sorry."

"Stonewall," my mother chimes in, "if you were sorry, you wouldn't have done it. You've got to stop being so irresponsible."

I shrug. "Must be the ADD."

This is my favorite all-purpose excuse.

Earlier this year I got diagnosed with attention deficit disorder. At school in history class, I'd get to gazing out the window at the janitors and cafeteria ladies tossing garbage into some Dumpsters, and only the third "Stonewall!" from Ms. Sherk would snap me back into class to face her glare and the snickers of the other kids. It's weird because I do actually like history—as long as I'm not reenacting it—but somehow every little thing distracts me.

A few weeks of this, and my grades slipping from B- to C to D, and I found myself one day in the guidance counselor's office. Then a session with the counselor *and* my parents. Then a visit to this kooky psychiatrist. A few stupid tests and presto, I've got ADD and a prescription for Ritalin.

I mostly think it's all crap. Who isn't bored with seventh grade? But ADD does have its advantages. Like now I have an excuse when I don't want to do homework. Or when I "forget" to do something like mow the yard. Or when I forget to bring something. Like today.

"I didn't mean to forget it," I sigh, and look to the ground.

Just when I think they may go for it, my father grunts. "I notice you didn't *forget* your Game Boy."

Hearing this, I know I've lost the battle, but I'm going to go down swinging. "Priorities, I guess."

"Well, you're going to have a bugle for tomorrow. You'll have to go see if you can get one from the sutlers." He gets his wallet and pulls out three twenty-dollar bills. "And you WILL pay me back. You're buying this with your own money."

"But—"

"No, no buts," Dad snarls. "You'd better march yourself down there and you'd better hope you can get one."

I grab the money and stomp out of the tent toward Sutler's Row because I'm so mad, I have to stomp off somewhere. I wish there was a door to slam. I've been saving my money for a long time to buy my own TV and DVD player so I don't have to watch the History Channel with my parents every single night. Now I'm going to have to blow most of it on a stupid bugle, which, by the way, I hardly know how to play anyway.

CHAPTER TWO

SUTLER'S ROW sits on a small hill next to the field where my parents and the other reenactors have pitched their tents. The row is actually two lines of large canvas tents separated by a grassy lane, and it's where the sutlers (the Civil War name for salesmen) set up to sell a bunch of crap to idiots like my parents.

Sutler's Row is also the only place where *civilians* are allowed, as in normal people wearing normal clothes who come to reenactments for a couple of hours to "experience history" before going back to their air-conditioned homes and real food and TV.

Up ahead of me is one family whose mother is fingering a quilt for sale while the father nudges a kid my age and points at me and my uniform. Like I'm some history lesson. The kid stares at me, I stare back, and I know both of us are thinking the same thing: Get me back to my PlayStation.

I duck into the nearest tent. The name of the place is Millie's Mercantile, even though some annoying guy in a beard and black hat works the cash register. The place sells all sorts of shirts, uniforms, and hats that, according to a sign over the counter, are "microscopically indistinguishable from the original items worn by the soldiers themselves!"

Whatever. No bugles.

The next tent has got the real touristy stuff. T-shirts with Rebel flags, muskets, pistols and cheap-looking swords, a bunch of knives, and some Civil War books. Gee, I'm surprised they don't have the Civil War chess set from the Franklin Mint!

No luck with the next sutler or the next, and I'm starting to wonder which would be worse, finding a bugle and wasting my money on it or not finding one and getting another round of crap from my parents.

I reach the end of the row and am about to cross the lane to go down the other side when I hear a whoop of applause from a group of reenactors about twenty yards away to my left. They're gathered under a dead, rotted-out oak tree. At first I can't see what they're clapping about because their backs are to me. But rising just above their heads, I see a Confederate battle flag and a wide-brimmed black hat.

Now I hear the voice—low and shrill at the same time somehow. It can only be one man—Nathan Bedford Dupree.

"Seven score years ago, our forefathers fought a brave and glorious fight to preserve a cherished way of life," Dupree rumbles over the murmuring crowd. "It is fitting that we gather here today to pay homage to their struggle."

"Senator" Dupree, as a lot of reenactors call him, is this tall, sunburned lawyer who made a bundle suing my favorite restaurant, Burger Boy, because some loser (probably a reenactor) says he got fat from eating five Bonanza Burgers a week.

Then he used that money to run two million annoying commercials on TV because he was trying to get elected to the state senate. Thankfully, he lost big-time.

But my parents think he's this great man who sticks up for the little guy even though it's Dupree, not "the little guy," driving the Mercedes.

I should say *drove* the Mercedes, since he lost it all last year after the IRS busted him for tax fraud. These days, Dupree drives an old Ford pickup from one reenactment to the next saying the same nonsense every time about the evils of the federal government and the glory of the South while trying to raise money to run for office again.

I've heard this speech a thousand times already. He starts it softly, sounding like your grandfather, making you listen hard to hear him. Not that I still do.

"And yet I wonder what would have happened had our forefathers prevailed," Dupree whispers loudly to the hushed crowd. "If instead of being forced at gunpoint back into that melting pot—*boiling pot,* if you ask me—of the United States of America, a new nation had been forged that shared a common language, faith, and heritage."

Here it comes—when the kind grandfather becomes the fiery preacher. I still can't see him, but I know his red face turns to blood, and he's about to pull out his latest prop. Sure enough, I see his black sleeve shoot up over the crowd. It's holding a tattered Bible.

"A country of decency, courtesy, and respect. Where our children had two parents—one man and one woman. Where they didn't walk around in gangs with their baggy pants and rap music and bad morals.

"But you and I, friends, we may come from all walks of life, but we are bound by a brotherhood. By the same proud heritage. We are a people of honor, our destinies bound to God and home and history. Yes, brothers. It is time to rise up. The fight for our heritage is upon us!"

The crowd goes nuts, but I'm not impressed. *What heritage?* Uncle Cyrus got shot in the butt! And the history's over, pal. And your side lost.

Dupree continues, "I have several books and brochures for sale, including my recent *The South is Rising Again!* which irrefutably proves . . ."

I turn away in disgust and walk right into someone who knocks my kepi over my eyes. All I see is the hem of a dress and a white apron. Right away I say, "Pardon, ma'am," which I know sounds real corny, but now that the reenactment has officially started I've got to talk period-style too. Sound like fun yet?

"It's cool," I hear. "No big deal."

I push my cap up to see who's the farby. Standing there is a girl about my age with a Confederate nurse's hat covering her bushy brown hair. She has these dark brown eyes, a lot of freckles, and a big smile. Oh crap, it's *the* girl! The one I've been talking about, the one I'm afraid to talk to.

I feel a nervous twist in my stomach. She is by far the coolest thing I've seen at a reenactment in a long time. And so what do I say to her?

14

"Sorry, I was looking for a place to puke," I mutter.

It was on the tip of my tongue. I couldn't help it. But she doesn't seem to mind.

"You mean because of that guy?"

"Yeah, I hate him," I whisper.

"At least you're not related to him," she says. "Like I am."

"You don't mean you're related to Dupree," I say.

She nods. "Yep, that's my dad, the Rebel without a brain."

And I thought my dad was bad. We watch as the crowd presses in on Dupree to buy his booklets.

"He hasn't always been this bad," the girl says quietly to me. She unties and ties the apron strings around her waist. "You've read all the stuff about him in the papers?"

I don't say anything. I don't know how to answer her, which is an answer itself, I guess. Even though she's not looking at me but down at her apron, she nods.

"So you know," she says. "He used to be an okay guy . . . sure, an obnoxious lawyer but a decent dad. But after the tax stuff and jail . . . "

"Jail?" I say loud enough for one sutler to turn our way.

I immediately regret it. The girl shrugs, but her eyes glisten. Perfect. Finally I've found a girl willing to talk to me and I'm making her cry!

"Only thirty days," she says. "But he came out changed somehow. Angrier. Meaner. Not to me and Mom too much, but to the world. I mean, he's always been a Civil War buff, but he started spending a lot of time on his computer surfing these *Heritage Not Hate* websites and visiting these old museums and researching his genealogy like he's some descendant

15

of Robert E. Lee. He even started his own blog, *The Rebel Yell*, where he and all these other nut jobs go on and on about the federal government and if only the South had won the war and Yankees *this* and blacks *that*."

I whistle.

"You're telling me," she says. "I can't even bring Maria, who's like my best friend at school, home anymore because she's black and he's got all these Confederate flags and junk hanging all over the place. And you wouldn't believe what he puts in those booklets."

"So now he's got you coming to reenactments," I say.

"I want to come," she says. "To keep an eye on him. I'm worried about him."

Man, she is really messed up. I don't say anything for a second, trying to think of some way to make her smile again, not cry.

"Let me ask you something," I finally say. "Do reenactments bite as hard as I think they do or am I just a big whiner?"

She cracks a smile and just as quick her big brown eyes dry up.

"Well, I'm getting the impression that, yes, you are a big whiner. But reenactments certainly do bite. My friends are all at Barnes and Noble right now drinking Chococinnos. When I get back they'll all have new clothes or boyfriends or they'll have all seen some movie together and won't be able to shut up about it. And I'll be like, 'Duh, I watched a guy pretend to shoot another guy.'"

At last! A sane person at a reenactment. A beautiful sane person. I think I'm falling in love.

It suddenly occurs to me that I've been talking to this beautiful girl longer than I've talked to any girl in a long time. But on one side of the lane I notice a sutler packing up for the night, and I still haven't found what I came here to get.

"Uh, I gotta go get a bugle," I say.

"Oh, are you a bugle boy?" she asks.

Oh man, that hurts! I feel my face get hot. "Kinda," I say.

But she's not laughing. "And you can play it?"

I shrug. "Good enough if you don't mind taps sounding exactly like the Hokey Pokey."

She laughs and touches my arm. No girl ever touches my arm! No girl ever laughs at my jokes! I know I'm in love.

"Ashby!"

We look to the crowd and there's Dupree, waving and yelling at her. "Ashby!"

The girl turns to look at him. "I'd better go," she says.

"Wait a second," I say. "Your name is Ashby? As in Turner Ashby? The Civil War general?"

She sighs. "I told you my dad has always been a Civil War buff. But if you would, please call me Ash."

"Gladly," I say. "Ash, you're not going to believe this . . . " For the first time in my life I'm glad to say it. "My name is Stonewall."

"No freaking way!"

Before I know it, she's gone.

I look around and see that most of the sutlers have packed up by now.

17

But I see one tent with the flap open. Standing in the opening is a big guy who, believe it or not, looks just like a real Civil War general. Bushy beard, wrinkled, sunburned face, and fierce blue eyes.

He's kind of scary, but I don't have many options left. I walk over to ask him about a bugle, but he starts talking first.

"Whew, I'm glad that big-mouthed poltroon Dupree finally shut up," the big guy says.

"Yeah, somebody really ought to do something about him," I say.

The big guy stares right at me with his scary eyes and says, "How about you, soldier?"

"Uh, I meant somebody else like, uh, I don't know," I babble. It's hard to think with this guy staring at me. I feel like I'm being inspected or something. "Are you still open?"

"For you I am."

"Oh good, uh, thanks, sir."

"Sir," he says softly and wrinkles his nose like he's sniffing the word. "I like that. But you really don't know who I am?"

I know you're a weirdo, I think. But I glance over at the phony-looking sutler sign on his tent. It says *Tom's Emporium.*

"I'm guessing you're Tom."

"At your service."

He sweeps aside the tent flap with one arm. That's when I realize that he's only got one arm. His other arm is not there at all and his sleeve is pinned to his shirt.

He catches me staring at it. "Old war wound," he says.

"I bet that hurt," I say.

He shrugs. "Being shot is not the worst thing that can happen to you," he says.

But the missing arm isn't as surprising as his clothes. No Civil War costume for this guy. He wears shorts, tube socks, flip-flops, and a faded, ripped tie-dyed T-shirt. Trust me, you don't see a lot of tie-dye at Civil War reenactments.

"C'mon in," he says. "I've been waiting on you."

Did he just say what I think he said? What is he, Count Dracula or something? That sounds like a signal for me to run for my life, but instead I find myself standing there like Victim #1.

"C'mon," he says, "I've got a sale on bugles."

Did I tell him I was looking for a bugle? That sounds like another signal for me to get out of here, but I'm herded inside before I can run screaming.

Right away, I notice that Tom's Emporium seems bigger than the other sutlers' tents even though from the outside his tent looks the same size. It's airier. I almost expect my voice to echo. When he drops the tent flap behind me, all other noises are silenced, like I've just shoved cotton balls in my ears. I hear the grass crunch beneath my feet as I walk around the tent.

Canteens and packs hang from tent poles. Uniforms and hats line one wall. Muskets and real sabers line another. He's got some old medical equipment displayed in a glass case. And there before me in the middle of the tent is a table filled with musical instruments. Drums, piccolos and fifes, a banjo, and several bugles.

No price tag of course. These people never seem to put

prices on anything. They're probably ashamed of how much they're ripping you off.

"How much are the bugles?"

By now Tom is reclining in a metal folding chair in the corner. He's holding a lemon in his mouth and with a knife in his one hand, he cuts the fruit in two. He offers me half but I shake my head. He shrugs and starts sucking on it.

"You shouldn't choose an instrument by the price tag, son."

I explain how I already have a perfectly good bugle at home, but I forgot it and my dad is making me buy a new one, so I'm looking for the cheapest thing I can find.

"It's surprising. You're a real conscript, aren't you?" he says, laughing. But it's a friendly laugh and I actually smile. I kind of like Tom. He says weird stuff, but he doesn't seem as phony as most of these sutlers and reenactors.

"What do you mean by conscript?" I ask.

"Well, a conscript was a soldier who didn't want to be a soldier. But they couldn't pay the bounty to get out of the army, so they had to go. Their hearts weren't in it. Like yours isn't, and you'd be glad to desert if you got the chance."

Conscript. Now that's a word I could appreciate. "My parents make me come. I think the Civil War is stupid and replaying it is twice as stupid."

"Hmmm," says Tom. He dumps the lemon rind in a can, stands, and walks to the table. He picks up one of his bugles. It's a real shiny one and I can see Tom's warped reflection in the brass. "Replaying it. Some would say we aren't replaying it at all, some would say it is still being played."

Suddenly Tom isn't so cool. Now he's sounding like my

dad, getting all mystic about the past. I reach out and take the bugle from him and blow a feeble *Charge!*

"This one works," I say. I take out my father's money. "How much?"

But Tom gives me another hard look.

"If I didn't know better, I'd say you're a pretty lousy bugle boy."

"That about sums it up," I say, "so I'll take your lousiest, cheapest bugle."

He laughs again. You know how some people laugh and you can tell they're dumb? Well, when Tom laughs I can tell he's smart. Real smart.

"Just a moment," he says.

He walks to the corner of his tent. On the floor is an old trunk. Unlike Tom's outfit, this trunk looks like the real thing. He opens it and digs around. I can't see what's inside because his body is blocking me. But when he stands and turns around, he is holding an old bugle with a tattered leather strap. At least it looks pretty old—a couple of dents, tarnished, dirty.

"I tell you what," he says. "Doesn't seem right that a conscript should have to pay his own way. How about I loan you this for the weekend. No charge, but you've got to promise to bring it back. And be careful with it. It's a valuable instrument."

"Really?" I say. "That's awesome, 'cause I'm saving up for my own TV."

"I guess that's good," says Tom, looking confused.

He hands me the bugle. I bring it up to my lips and blow

Charge! It sounds even crappier than on mine at home. Dad's going to love this. But at least it's free.

Tom smiles. "I bet it'll sound a whole lot better tomorrow. Oh and look, I've got some instructions for it."

He turns back to the trunk.

"I really don't think I'll need the instructions," I say. "I already know how . . ."

He turns back around with a big ratty book. He pulls out some folded-up papers that were stuck in there like a bookmark.

"Good, because these instructions are old and a bit fragile too, so don't bother with them unless you really need them. Just keep 'em in your pocket."

And he shoves the paper into the breast pocket of my uniform. Whatever. For a free bugle, I guess I can play along with whatever this guy's delusion is.

I thank him a lot and promise to take good care of it.

"I'm not real worried about the bugle," says Tom, now sounding really serious. "Make sure you take care of yourself."

I turn and open the tent flap and there again is Senator Dupree's voice. He's back to being a grandfather, silky and smooth, as he shakes the hands of the people in the crowd— my beaming parents among them now, I see.

"And watch out for that guy," Tom says.

CHAPTER THREE

OH YEAH, did I mention that the food sucks? For supper we have some terrible soup with half-raw vegetables my mom cooked in a black pot over the fire. After I barely sleep all night because the ground is rocky and the yahoos at the next campfire drink moonshine and whoop Rebel yells all night, we have leftover soup for breakfast. Luckily I've smuggled in some Pop-Tarts.

I now find myself hunkered down in a field with my dad and a whole herd of Confederate reenactors. It's early morning and the sun has just cleared the trees—a time most kids my age are still asleep or watching SpongeBob reruns in their pajamas. The grass is dewy and my pants are so damp I feel like I've peed myself. I seriously wish I was watching the SpongeBob reruns.

We are waiting for the Yankee reenactors to make their charge. They are about a hundred yards away from us across a small stream.

Both sides are in the exact positions they were on July 21,

1861, when the real battle began, but I doubt the Confederates back then were as out of shape as Dad's friends. And I don't think they would have patiently waited for half an hour for the Yankees—who seem to be in even worse shape—to waddle into formation. Whoopee! History comes alive!

You might be confused and think this is exciting. It's not. I've snored my way through this reenactment so many times I know it by heart. This general goes there, his men follow, then they go there, then they die. Etc., etc. The upshot is that I know much, much more about this stupid battle than I want to.

Basically, these Southern states had seceded from the United States to start their own country, the Confederate States. Real original name, guys! President Lincoln didn't want this to happen, so he sent Union troops from Washington to capture Richmond, Virginia, which was the capital of the Confederacy.

But they only got thirty miles away from Washington when they ran into Confederate troops near the town of Manassas at a stream called Bull Run. Everybody in Washington figured it would be a pretty quick battle, and lots of bigwigs actually followed the Union army in carriages just to watch. (Is that sick or what?)

Of course, just to add to the authenticity of our weekend, the reenactment of the Battle of First Manassas is not actually on the Manassas battlefield. The real battlefield is owned by the federal government, which for some crazy reason doesn't want a bunch of wackos dressed up in Civil War uniforms marching around its land.

So the few hundred people here for the reenactment have

pitched their tents on a private farm next to the real battle-field. Our campsite is right along Bull Run near a place called Sudley Springs Ford where the Union army crossed the stream to first attack the Rebels.

This is what we're waiting for now. Across the stream are maybe three hundred Yankees, a far cry from the thousands who actually attacked. Of course, the real Confederate army had ten times the number in our group. Real authentic.

"Can't you just feel it, Stonewall?" Dad whispers. He's wearing his "farmer's reenactment garb," white shirt, home-spun britches, and straw hat, which is what most Confeder-ates would have worn that early in the war before they got real uniforms. Real geeky.

Not that I look any better. For some reason, because I'm a bugle boy, Dad figures I would have had a uniform. So I've got on a hot and itchy pair of light blue pants and matching jacket with a yellow bandanna around my neck that makes me look like a Cub Scout reject. (Underneath it all is my trade-mark *Are We Having Fun Yet?* T-shirt—not much of a protest, but what can I say.) I've got this satchel over my shoulder that looks like a purse, which at least gives me a place to stash my Game Boy in case I get a chance to sneak away. Thankfully, the guys from school have never seen me in this getup. And hopefully they never will.

"Stonewall! I asked if you could feel it?"

Uh-oh, I can see he feels like bonding.

"What?" I ask.

He sighs and a dreamy look spreads over his face. "It feels like we're actually there. It's magical."

25

Much more of this magical crap and I don't care what they do to me, I will not come back.

"Pardon me, gents," says a voice over my shoulder.

Oh, great, just what I need to make the day perfect. Here comes Senator Dupree again! He barges in right next to me and starts combing his goatee and straightening his black hat. Now all eyes are on him.

"I'm feeling good about today, boys," he calls out. "This war will be ours before the day is done."

Well, duh, Dupree. It's not like we don't know that the Confederates win today, though saying the war will be ours is a bit much since they got their butt beat in the end.

He loads his rifle as well as this tiny little pistol that couldn't kill a rat, much less a reenactor. He holsters it on his ankle—the whole time yakking away about the destiny of the South.

Luckily, after a few minutes he wanders off. I hear him yammering as he walks the line. Reenactors nod as he passes. He reaches the very end of the line, but instead of stopping he keeps walking right into the woods, where he disappears behind a tree. Either he forgot to use the Porta-John or he's kinda creepy. Maybe both.

"Hi, Stonewall!"

I turn around to find Ash strolling toward me. It's pretty unusual for a female reenactor to be in this part of the battle-field, so everybody turns to look. I notice even a few Yankee reenactors watching. Some reenactors get all prissy, because she isn't supposed to be here. My dad is one of these people. I can practically hear him *tsk, tsk*-ing.

But she seems oblivious to the looks she's attracting. "Stonewall! Have you seen my dad?"

I try to act cool too, despite the neckerchief and a thousand other things that make me uncool. But I feel the glare of my father and all the others and can only manage a whisper. "Yeah, Ash, he went that way."

I manage to cut my eyes at my dad and give Ash an eye roll. I lean closer and whisper, "I really hate this."

Ash leans close to me and says right back, "Then why are you here?"

"What choice do I have?"

She puts her fingertip to her chin. "Well . . . you could *choose* to get shot as soon as possible. You could choose to require immediate medical attention and go to the hospital, where a particular nurse could choose to hang out with you the rest of the day."

"Really?"

"Sure," she says with a really nice smile.

Man, this could be the best reenactment ever.

Suddenly, the Yankee bugler blows and a drum starts to beat. Ash glances across the springs. "I guess that's my cue. Let me go find my dad real quick." As she runs off she yells over her shoulder, "See you soon!"

I watch her run behind the line. At the end I spot Dupree, who's reemerged from the woods and is now kneeling on the ground like he's tying his shoe. No wonder Ash needs to keep an eye on him.

I look across the springs. In two long battle lines, one behind the other, the Yankees begin marching toward us.

Bring 'em on! Let's get this battle started! One shot! That's all I need to hear and I'm down. Down!

The Union guys are struggling through the stream.

"Stonewall!" Dad says. "Are you ready?"

Here we go. I look down our line to my left and see Mr. Harvey sitting on his white horse. Mr. Harvey has white hair and a long white beard and is playing Colonel Nathan Evans today. The real Colonel Evans, whose nickname was "Shanks" because his legs were so skinny, was the fierce Confederate commanding officer at that moment in the real Battle of Bull Run. Earlier that morning, the real Colonel Evans had figured out that a small Union attack three miles away was just a diversion to keep the Confederates from the real attack here at Sudley Springs. He was able to rush his troops to Sudley Springs just in time.

Mr. Harvey, our Colonel Evans, isn't so fierce. He really owns a dry cleaner's, has terrible breath, and legs that aren't even close to skinny. But he gets to play Colonel Evans every year because July 21 is his birthday. Happy birthday, Mr. Harvey.

Mr. Harvey slowly draws his sword. All the men in our line raise their muskets and aim them at the Yankees.

"Stonewall!" Dad snaps.

Oh yeah, the bugle. I'm so anxious to get wounded, I almost forgot. I raise it up, trying to look a little bit like I actually know how to use it. Suddenly I realize I never practiced playing it since Tom gave it to me. Now I'm definitely not feeling magical. The mouthpiece will be cold and I know I won't get a sound out. And I know that, to Dad, a poorly played *Charge!* will almost be as bad as me not having a bugle at all.

But when the bugle touches my lips I have to jerk it away because the metal is so hot. I look and see the dents ripple and smooth out. And the rust and dirt tarnishing the surface fade away, leaving the horn gleaming and spotless in the morning sun.

"Dad? Look at—"

"Stonewall! Shhhh!" he hisses. "Just be ready."

"But Dad—"

Ringing out over the field is the voice of Mr. Harvey, who shakily points his sword at the Yankees and croaks, "Charge."

"Now, Stonewall!" cries Dad. "Now!"

Without thinking, I put my mouth to the bugle. The metal is like fire. I take a deep breath, close my eyes, and blow.

CHAPTER FOUR

I'VE ALWAYS hated it in movies when somebody goes back in time and it takes them half of the movie to stop saying "I must be dreaming."

No, you know right away.

At least I do.

A sunny, blue sky just a few moments ago is now filled with clouds. The short grass under my feet has become knee-high weeds and thistles. Scrubby trees have sprouted here and there.

The annoying hum of the interstate is gone, replaced by gunfire and screams. And louder than anything else—my own bugle blasting out a loud, clear note like I have never played before.

"Charge!" cries a voice. I look. Standing in the stirrups on a white horse is a wild-eyed officer with a kooky Amish-looking beard waving his sword over his head. It has to be the real Colonel Evans. It sure ain't Mr. Harvey!

Am I freaked out? Of course I'm freaked out. Reenactments may be boring, but at least they're predictable—pretend to charge, pretend to shoot, pretend to die. But there's no pretend about this. I can actually hear bullets buzzing over my head. I look down. There's a guy on the ground in front of me holding his bloody stomach and trying to keep his insides from spilling out. I throw up all that leftover soup I ate for breakfast.

I've got to get out of here. Out of this real battle and back to the fake one. Being with my dad's friends never seemed so good. But how, I don't know, and there's no time to stand around like a dipwad talking about dreaming. I've got to move or I'm toast.

Someone suddenly shoves me from behind.

"Look out, boy!" a big bushy-bearded man roars. He jostles past me, almost knocking me down. I turn around in time to see another man raising his rifle to push me to the side. "Durn fool!" he shouts. Behind him come even more men.

I glimpse another officer on horseback, waving his sword and shouting, "Move, men, move!"

They swarm past me. Eager and angry.

Instead of a bunch of pasty, middle-aged guys in costumes, this is a mob of tough, lean men. Real soldiers. Or at least real farmers in a real war. They look like they just dropped their pitchforks in the field, picked up a rifle, and came here to fight. Many don't have uniforms, they aren't marching in a straight line. And they stink. Body odor, and I mean bad. I am surrounded by men who have been marching for days without a bath or fresh clothes.

And they really want to fight! Each guy is pushing hard

to get to the front of the line, like he wants to fire the first shot. Which is real inconvenient since I'm pushing hard in the opposite direction. Retreat! Retreat!

But I can't turn back. Another man shoves me and I stumble forward. I have to start running or the mass of men will trample me. Instead of the stutter-steps of the reenactors, these men really move.

In the middle of this pack of war-crazed soldiers, I can't see where we're going and I can't stop. At times we're pressed so close that I feel like I could pick up my feet and be carried along.

I hear a *crack, crack, crack.* The pack of men stops, separates. Between the shoulders of the men in front of me I see rank on rank of Union soldiers about seventy-five yards ahead. They've just crossed the stream, but they don't seem real organized either. They're clumped up in groups instead of one solid line of battle.

But they look like they want this too. And enough seem to know how to aim their guns and fire, because a couple of men in front of me suddenly crumple to the ground.

Watching them writhe in real pain, with real blood spurting out of real wounds, I realize I'm in real danger. I'm sure a bullet will hurt me just as bad as any of these men.

I'm still clutching my bugle. If it got me into this mess, maybe it can get me out. I put it to my mouth, but now the metal is cold. I give a little toot. Nothing happens. I blow harder. Still nothing. I try blowing *Charge!* again.

"You maggot spawn!" says a redheaded soldier as he slaps the bugle from my mouth. "We're already charging! Stop blowing that durn bugle and get ready to fight!"

He rushes on ahead, like the other soldiers around me. There's no real formation, no real direction. Soldiers scramble everywhere trying to get a good shot. Trying to chase after the Yankees, who I can't see anymore.

There's a huge explosion to my left. Dirt and pebbles sting my face and I fall to the ground. It must have been an artillery shell. I look to where it hit and almost puke. Lying just a few feet from me is a ripped-up soldier. His left leg is gone. I can tell right away that even in a modern hospital he wouldn't have much of a chance.

I crawl to him and try to hide behind his dead body for cover. His face is gray and speckled with dirt.

His eyes open, and I scream.

"Take my gun," he wheezes. "It's loaded. Take it!"

The gun is as tall as me and feels as heavy, and I can't imagine being able to even aim it, much less shoot it. I sling the bugle over my shoulder and take the gun. The man closes his eyes. I don't move, but try to will myself deeper in the ground.

Suddenly I feel a pain in my shin. I open my eyes and the dead man's looking at me again. And kicking me with his one good leg!

"Get!" he snarls.

It's either get up or get kicked. I get to my hands and knees and crawl out of kicking range.

The rest of the Confederates have run past, but are now being pushed back toward us. I can see Union men in the swarm now. They have gone past the stage of firing guns. They're too close to take the time to reload. But they're not too close to use their bayonets. I've read all about this in Dad's books and I know a bayoneting is a bad wound. These blades attached to the barrel of a musket are designed to make you lose as much blood as possible, but I never knew it could be as bad as what I'm seeing.

Suddenly a Yankee is right on top of me. He's a freaking giant wearing a real U.S. Army uniform—a real soldier, not just some farmer with a gun. He's got an open gash running from his ear to his nose and is yelling his head off. I can't tell if he's angry or having the best day of his life. He stabs down at me with his bloody bayonet.

I roll just in time. The blade crunches into the ground an inch from my ear. I try to raise my gun. The Yankee's heavy black boot kicks it out of my hands and pins me down. He jerks the blade out of the ground and raises it for another strike.

The only thing I've got left is the bugle. I hold it feebly in front of me.

"No, don't!" I gasp. "I'm not really a soldier!"

He's not listening. He's laughing, his mouth twisting into a snarl. I close my eyes, brace for the bayonet.

A huge wet weight falls on my legs. I open my eyes. It's the Yankee. He's dead. Shot in the head. I look up to see the red-haired Confederate shaking his head at me. The guy who called me a maggot spawn. He looks at the bugle I'm still holding pathetically in front of me.

"Didn't I tell you to drop that durn thing and fight?"

I squirm out from underneath the Yankee. My pants are soaked in his blood.

"You owe me one, brother," he says. He crouches down and reloads his musket. "Didn't expect it to be so *intense*. That's the word, don't you think? And the noise! My stars! I've never heard so much in my entire life. Talk about sound and fury!"

He prattles away until a cheer from the Yankees interrupts him. We both look up and see away to our right a Confederate flag-bearer fall to his knees. He tries planting the staff into the ground as he falls. It stays upright and looks like it will hold. But a breeze topples it onto him, the flag draping over the bearer's dead body.

Thirty yards beyond the fallen flag, a Yankee crouches low to the ground and starts running for the flag. He obviously hopes to capture it and be a war hero, but before he takes five steps, the red-haired guy who has just saved me has jumped over a bunch of bodies, almost gotten shot, and picked up the fallen flag.

My new-found friend holds it up and turns to face the rest of our brigade. "Yeeeehaaaaaaaa!" he cries. His back to the Yankees, he waves the flag over his head, oblivious to the gunfire now aimed right at him. Bullets pierce the flag and one breaks the staff just above his hand. But he catches the falling flag before it hits the ground. Again he starts waving and whooping, and now many of the other men let out whoops of their own. They start to push forward again.

For a second it looks like they're winning. They're actually driving the Yankees back. But one look over their heads and I see that the Yankees aren't really retreating. They're falling back into a storm of Union reinforcements who are marching right at us. A glance down our line tells me that we are about to be swamped.

"Fall back! To the hill, men!" cries Colonel Evans.

Finally, an order I can live with. I jump to my feet and pick up the heavy musket. Everybody who is left turns and runs for a cover of trees at the top of a hill behind us. Everybody but that redheaded lunatic still waving the flag. He finally starts running with us when he realizes we aren't coming back. The battle has only lasted about fifteen minutes and already I'm exhausted. But those trees look like safety and I run as fast as anyone.

"Take cover!" cries Colonel Evans. "Reload and prepare to hold the hill!" He gallops on to the edge of the trees, where I guess he can see what is happening.

I don't need to see. I already know. Unlike all the real soldiers here struggling to stay alive, I know everything that is going to happen today. As crazy as it sounds, all that worthless information my dad pumped into me is now actually useful.

As I flop down beside some of the other men under the trees, I know that we are on Matthews Hill. General Bee will be here soon with some reinforcements, but they won't be enough. We will fall back to Henry Hill and there will be my namesake, General Thomas J. "Stonewall" Jackson—though he hasn't gotten the nickname Stonewall yet. That's coming up soon.

I know that the battle is really just getting started. I know that by the end of the day, the Confederates will claim victory, but that almost a thousand men—maybe the men sitting next to me right now—will die.

I even know that my great-great-great-great-uncle will get shot in the butt, if he hasn't already.

I also know that I've got to get the heck out of here.

"Boy oh boy! Durn, this is something, ain't it?" someone says.

I look up. It's the redheaded guy again. He must really like the word *durn*. But he's grinning now. He has handed off the flag to someone in the color guard, and is reloading his gun while watching the Yankees at the bottom of the hill.

"Why did they make us retreat?" he mutters. "That was starting to get fun."

I look up at him. His red hair is fiery against the gray sky. Up close I see he's only a few years older than me. I guess I just assumed all these soldiers were grown men, but this guy looks like he could be one of the high school kids who ride my bus. He's leaner than me and much taller, but he's still got a few pimples and could definitely use braces if not a whole new set of teeth, I notice, as he cracks a big, crazy smile while pouring powder down the gun's long muzzle.

Somehow knowing that he's a kid too makes what happened on the battlefield even more embarrassing. "Thanks," I say. "You know . . . for what you did."

He finishes loading and sights his musket. "You mean for saving your durn life?" He smiles. "Don't mention it. You'd do the same for me. You'd *better* do the same for me or I'll come back to life and kick your butt! Ha! Just joshing you, brother. That'd make a good story though. I got to write that down." He drops his voice real low: "A man . . . haunted the rest of his life by the spirit of the man whose life he didn't save. *Oooooooooo. Double, double toil and trouble. Et tu, Brute?* Yes, I've got to write that down. What regiment are you from anyway? Ain't seen you before."

This dude is seriously off the wall. Talk about ADD. He could definitely use some of my Ritalin. It takes me a second to realize he's asked me a question, which I try to dodge.

"Well, I ain't seen you before either," I say, trying to match his accent.

"Good point." He extends his hand. "What's your name?"

We shake. His hand is hard as rocks. "Stonewall Hinkleman," I say and smile.

A surprised look shoots across his face. "Hot durn! That's the same as mine."

"Stonewall?" I ask. Since Stonewall Jackson hasn't gotten his nickname yet, I figured I'd be the only one.

"Nah," says the kid. "Hinkleman. That's me. Cyrus Hinkleman."

The smile slips from my face. My stomach lurches.

"Whoa!" he says. "You look like you've seen a ghost."

I have.

CHAPTER FIVE

IT'S GOOD that I have something to think about besides all the people I just saw get shot and stabbed. A few feet away from me, a young guy with freckles and blond hair is trying to load his gun, but his hands shake too badly and all his powder spills onto the ground. He tries to scoop up the black powder and pour it back down the barrel, all the while talking to himself. It's obvious all he can think about is dying, and he probably will.

Frankly, that's all that I've been thinking about so far. I've been mocking my dad and all his reenactor buddies for years. I should have been paying attention! Knowing about the Civil War isn't enough. I need to know how to *act* in it. Like what to do with this musket I've got in my hands. I'm glad it's already loaded, because after I fire that one shot I'm screwed!

But now my brain races in another direction. Thinking of bits and pieces of movies and science fiction books I have read. If there's one thing I've learned, you can't mess around in the past without messing up the future. One wrong step and your parents never meet, or you never get born, or apes rule the world, or Michael J. Fox has to play the guitar real loud.

Or your great-great-great-great-uncle survives the war's first battle and goes on to be Robert E. Lee's right-hand man and single-handedly destroys the Union Army two years later at Gettysburg, winning the war for the South.

Maybe that's a stretch. I don't think I've done anything yet to keep Cyrus from getting shot. I do feel like a jackass for all the cracks I've made about him. He seems like a real nice guy, and he's the exact opposite of a coward.

I mean, right now he's got this stone in his hand that he uses to sharpen these two knives that he keeps in a scabbard on each hip.

"Nice knives," I say.

Cyrus flips one out of his belt, lets it spin in the air a couple of times, and catches it by the hilt.

"Is this a dagger I see before me?" he says, doing his crazy Shakespeare thing again. He could almost be one of those drama geeks from school. But then he says, "Not really a dagger, actually, a throwin' knife. And I got a pretty good arm, if you don't mind me bragging a little."

He looks down the hill, to where some Yankees are gathered about a hundred yards away.

"Heck, I could probably stick one of 'em between the eyes from here. Well . . . maybe."

Okay, so he's not exactly like the drama geeks. A little more . . . uh, violently insane. But . . . he did save my life.

Speaking of life-saving, my main mission is to survive this

battle and get the heck out of here. The best thing I can do is run away, lay low, and try to figure out how to make this bugle take me back home.

I give the bugle a quick try. I bring it to my lips and play the first thing that comes to mind—the opening of "Dixie," better known as the *Dukes of Hazzard* car horn song.

The metal stays cold, and I stay where I am.

"Whew," says Cyrus, "you mean you been carrying that thing around all day and that's the best you can play it?"

Cyrus turns back to look down the hill at the Yankees who are getting into formation. No one's watching me. This is as good a time as any to slink away. I know the battle will pass this hill in a little while. Maybe I can just hide until everyone moves on. There's a fallen tree about twenty yards behind our line. If I can just make it to there, I should be able to sit out the rest of the battle. Then I can concentrate on getting back.

Just as I am getting ready to run, someone barks, "You two! I need two fast runners."

"Yes, sir," calls Cyrus eagerly, pulling me to my feet.

The order has come from an officer. It's Colonel Evans, and Cyrus seems anxious to please him.

"Our signal boys are missing," Colonel Evans says. "I need you two to take a message to General Bee."

"Yes, sir!" chirps Cyrus happily.

This sounds great. If I can't hide behind a tree, at least I'll be running away from the action.

But as Colonel Evans hands Cyrus the message, another thought occurs to me. "What happened to the other signal boys?" I ask.

41

Colonel Evans doesn't answer. From the look on his face, he doesn't have to. Those boys aren't missing. They're already dead. Messengers make easy targets for Yankee sharpshooters.

From where we're standing on Matthews Hill, Colonel Evans points out Bee's men. They're about half a mile away on top of Henry Hill, beside a two-story white building that has to be the Henry House. It might as well be thirty miles away. The land between the two hills is an open hay field. Separating the hills is a wide dirt road known as the Warrenton Turnpike and Young's Branch, a creek that flows into Bull Run. A brick house by the turnpike and a few trees along Young's Branch are the only protection from Yankee sharpshooters and cannons pouring fire on us.

It's hard to believe these guys had to go through this much trouble to send a message half a mile. I'm going to be really ticked off if I get killed because Colonel Evans didn't have a cell phone.

"Get going!" roars Colonel Evans. "You tell Bee to either send more men up here or expect us to fall back to that hill where he's standing. Now go! Go!"

Cyrus takes off like a freaked-out rabbit. I'm right behind him, realizing that the faster we run the safer we will be. I hope this isn't where Cyrus gets his butt shot, because then I'll be out there all alone.

For a moment, no one seems to be shooting at us. I look around as we run down Matthews Hill and notice that except for a stray cannonball every now and then, we aren't in the line of Yankee fire.

We scramble through the field and pass by the brick house, which I recognize as the Stone House from my many trips to the battlefield park with dad. We cross the Warrenton Turnpike and wade through Young's Branch.

Cyrus must be in good shape, because he's still going strong. Me, I'm panting and wheezing. The only time I've ever run this far was in gym class, and it took me the whole period to make it. But now I'm too scared to fall behind.

We come out of the trees lining the creek and start up Henry Hill when suddenly to our right we see two old ladies in dusty dresses carrying an even older lady on a mattress. They stumble. The old lady almost falls to the ground. She cries out, and I can see that all three women are terrified.

"What the heck?" says Cyrus, who is, of course, completely surprised by this. I'm confused for a second too, until it dawns on me it has to be old Mrs. Judith Henry.

I hesitate, not sure what to do. I know that Mrs. Henry, whose house sits on Henry Hill, is not going to live through the day. By pure coincidence, her house, out of the thousands and thousands in Virginia, is where these two massive armies fight their first battle.

"No, no, take me back to the house!" cries the old lady.

"But it's not safe!" says one of her helpers.

"Don't care!" says the old lady. "I want to die in my own bed!"

According to the history books, that's exactly where she does die. But as the two women struggle to pick up the mattress again, a stray shell hits the field by the stream.

The explosion rattles our teeth and the two women scream, dropping the old lady a second time.

For some reason, this is the most messed-up thing I've seen all day. I always thought war was about the soldiers, not about little old ladies. Still, history is history. I'm sorry her final hours are going to be so crazy and scary, but if she wants to die in her own bed there's nothing we can do to save her.

I start running toward General Bee . . . only to find Cyrus running toward the ladies!

"Cyrus!" I yell. "It's not going to matter!"

He stops and turns to me with this strange look on his face. Suddenly, the women scream again and point behind us. Horses and riders head our way at full gallop. If they're Yankees, we're all dead. But no, I can see now that they are Confederates. As they come closer, I can see that one looks familiar, a general maybe, with a dark pointed goatee and broad-rimmed hat.

The general begins shouting long before he gets his horse stopped.

"Quick, boys, are you Evans's men? Where is he?"

"Holding a position at the top of that hill, sir," answers Cyrus.

"Wait!" Cyrus cries as the rider spurs his horse to keep galloping. "He's sent us with a message. Are you General Bee?"

"Yes, yes, of course, for God's sake hurry!"

Cyrus hands him the scrap of paper. I blurt out, "Colonel Evans can't hold the hill. He needs more men or he has to retreat to Henry Hill."

"What hill?" General Bee asks.

That's right. It's not named Henry Hill yet. The naming of things comes after the fighting. I point to Mrs. Henry's house.

There's a flicker of defeat in General Bee's eyes. He wasn't looking for more bad news.

"Miller, ride back, warn Capshaw!" One of the riders spurs his horse into a tight turn and gallops off.

"Anything else?" Bee asks us.

"Do you want us to take Colonel Evans a message, sir?" asks Cyrus.

"No, I'll go myself!" shouts Bee, and spurs his own horse across the stream and road we just crossed and races toward Evans's men, who even now are retreating down Matthews Hill.

"Come on," Cyrus says. "The battle is going to reach this spot any minute. We've got to help the old woman!"

Even though the hot July sun burns brightly outside, inside Mrs. Henry's house is dim and gray as we step through the front door.

Sweat drips from our faces as we lug the old woman into the parlor. Mrs. Henry's face shines with sweat too, but her skin is so white from sickness or fear—I'm not sure which—she looks like a wet piece of marble. We lay her down.

"Oh, Margaret, Margaret," she wails. The two women rush inside and lean the muskets they've been carrying for us by the door. Margaret comes forward to take Mrs. Henry's hand.

After being outside all day I can barely see in here.

45

"Where's the light switch?" I ask.

The other woman gives me a puzzled look. She goes to the window and swishes aside a curtain. Sunlight streams inside.

Right. No electricity. No lightbulbs. Just sun. Mom and Dad would love this place. Real authentic.

"Her bedroom is this way," says Ms. Margaret, and she starts climbing a rickety staircase.

Upstairs. Of course it is. Cyrus goes first and I have to raise my end to keep Mrs. Henry level so she won't slide off the mattress. She's heavier than she looks.

"Jacob!" the other woman calls. Out of a dim corner comes a black kid about my age. He wears raggedy overalls and no shoes. He glances at me as he takes one handle of the mattress and I'm surprised to see that, even in the house's dim lighting, his eyes are the greenest I've ever seen.

"Thanks," I say.

He looks confused and just as quick, his eyes dart back to the ground. At first I think he's shy. But halfway up the stairs it hits me. He's not shy. He's a slave. At my school, we could be on the forensics club together, but here in 1861 he's just a slave.

We hoist Mrs. Henry into her room. Her room has a dresser, a big bowl that must be a washbasin, a wooden chair in one corner, and a low bed in the other. A Bible sits on a small table next to the bed.

Out the window I can see the Confederates retreating across Young's Branch and up Henry Hill. Across the turnpike in the hay field, two solid lines of Union soldiers are advancing.

We carefully ease the mattress onto Mrs. Henry's bed.

"Ohhhh," she moans. The women arrange her black dress and pull a blanket to her chest. Her white knuckles clench the blanket.

"She's got the fever," says Ms. Margaret.

The other woman picks up the washbasin. "Jacob. Go get some water and towels."

"Yes, ma'am," the boy says and leaves the room.

"And send word for your father," she calls after him.

A voice rumbles from the stairway. "No need for that."

I turn to the doorway. Materializing out of the stairway's darkness is a tall black man—another of Mrs. Henry's slaves, I assume. He is bald and seems old too, judging by the wrinkles in his face. But his walk is strong and steady as he crosses the room to Mrs. Henry's side. The two other women step aside to let him pass.

"What you need now, Missus Henry?" he asks.

She holds out a trembling hand to him, which his large hands seem to swallow.

"Edward. Edward. They're coming."

A high-pitched scream rushes through the air. A crash rocks the house, knocking everyone but the black man to the floor. He almost goes over but bends his knees and sways like he's on a tossing ship, and he's able to steady himself.

Cyrus and I crawl to the window.

"Durn," he mutters.

The Confederate army is now almost to the house. Crossing the turnpike at the foot of Henry Hill is the Union army. Far behind it, on top of Matthews Hill, clouds of black smoke rise from half a dozen Union artillery guns firing cannon-balls right at us, like Mrs. Henry's house has a giant bull's-eye painted on it.

Several more explosions shake us. We look down and there below us, Confederate cannons are starting to fire at the oncoming Yankees.

"Mercy!" Cyrus shouts. "Have you ever seen such!" I elbow him and we both turn around. The women are still lying face-down on the floor, crying and hugging each other so tightly they look like one big mass of clothing and hair. The black man, now sitting on the edge of Mrs. Henry's bed, gazes at us with wide, unblinking eyes.

Jacob stumbles into the room carrying a large basin of water that he sets beside Mrs. Henry.

"Oh, Jacob, thank you," she says weakly. "It's such a comfort having both of you here."

Jacob smiles, but it's not a real smile. It's fake, like one he's practiced for a play.

The black man dips the towel in the water and places it over Mrs. Henry's forehead.

"I'll stay with Missus Henry. Y'all get on to the McLean place where it's safer," he says to the two women. He looks at Cyrus and me and adds, "Or wherever else you ought to be."

The two women go down the stairs first. Cyrus follows at a gallop.

I'm perfectly fine where I am. I've got four walls around me that are at least strong enough to stop a bullet. Maybe I could squeeze myself under her bed to be on the safe side.

"Get," the black man says. It's the second time I've heard that word today. Must be something in the air.

I look at him. His eyes are fierce, glaring at me.

I take a deep breath, get to my feet, and bolt for the door. I spin around to look for a final time at Mrs. Henry. I know that any minute now, a bullet or maybe an artillery shell is going to crash into her room and kill her. (So maybe this isn't the safest place to be!) She is supposed to be the only civilian killed in this battle. But I don't see how the black man is going to survive if he stays at her side. Maybe because he's a slave the history records won't count him as a person.

He's still holding Mrs. Henry's hand in one hand, but his other is on Jacob's shoulder. They look at each other for a long moment. The man nods and Jacob runs past me so quickly I can't tell if it is sweat or spilled water or tears on his cheeks. The man glances at me a moment and turns back to Mrs. Henry.

Another shell hits the house. Cyrus is probably already outside. I don't want to go back out to the battle, but I can't stay here. I know this place is going to get hit, and hard. Besides, there is nothing left to do for Mrs. Henry. She is going to die, but at least we got her back to her room.

I head down the stairs and out the door, and find that the battle has caught up with us.

CHAPTER SIX

CYRUS IS already in the new Confederate line of battle that extends out from either side of Mrs. Henry's house. Our artillery has stopped the Union troops cold. (I'm going to say "our" while they're keeping me from getting killed!) At the bottom of the hill, the Yankees are hiding behind the trees along Young's Branch to form a new battle line in the turnpike.

But they're not going to be pinned down long. Yankee reinforcements pour down Matthews Hill, while above them more Union artillery begins firing at us.

Maybe now's a good chance for me to bid Bull Run goodbye. It's been great, folks! The bullets, the slaughter, little old ladies scared to death!

Reenactments have never looked so good.

There's a wood of cedar trees about a quarter of a mile to the rear. Nothing but an open field separates me from its shelter—and promise of escape.

I step down from the porch to the yard and start walking away from the house, away from the Confederate line. Cyrus and everyone are all looking the other way, down the hill at the Yankees. I try to act casual in case anyone's looking. *Don't mind me . . . just taking a nice summer stroll through a battlefield . . . nothing to see here.* Just a few more steps and I can run for it.

"Stonewall!" someone calls. I can't keep myself from looking back.

It's Cyrus.

He's leaning on his musket and talking with two men—one tall and gangly, the other short and squat like a tree stump. Both are older than Cyrus, have curly black hair, thick beards, and pale faces that don't seem to smile often. They're both wiping blood off their faces.

Somehow this doesn't seem like a real classy moment to slink away and hide under a log. Reluctantly, I join them.

They're loading their muskets as I come up to them.

"There you are," I say when I reach Cyrus's side.

"Get ready, my friend," Cyrus says. "The Yanks are upon us, but here we'll make our stand! Once more into the breach!"

The two men beside him roll their eyes and shake their heads.

"This here's Big Jim and Elmer," Cyrus tells me. "They're brothers, live close to my daddy's farm back home. Boys, this is Stonewall Hinkleman."

Big Jim takes aim down the hill. "Didn't know you had kin, Cyrus," he says, his finger on the trigger. He fires and a cloud of smoke hides his face. Elmer does the same.

Cyrus scratches his head. "I haven't figured that one out

51

yet, Big Jim." Cyrus grins. "He's kind of hefty for a Hinkle-man, but he moves pretty quick when he needs to."

Big Jim and Elmer don't answer. They're busy reloading, and even though I know the basics, for the first time in my life I really pay attention. Forget all the junk about flank-ing maneuvers and sidearm shift and which side is right or wrong. I need to know how to really load this thing!

First, they tear a packet of powder with their teeth and pour the powder down the gun's barrel. They take the ramrod from the musket and pack down the powder, then drop in a round metal ball. They cock the hammer and set a firing cap under it.

Now they're ready to shoot—all in just fifteen seconds!

So when they pull the trigger, the hammer will strike the cap . . . which will shoot out a spark . . . which will touch off the gunpowder . . . which will fire the ball out of the gun . . . which, considering the technology of the early Civil War musket, will have a decent chance of hitting someone if they are less than a hundred yards away.

How on earth am I going to remember all that?

Big Jim and Elmer look down to the road at the foot of the hill, where the number of Yankees has grown so large they make the road look like a raging river. They sigh a deep breath, aim, and fire.

I look to Cyrus, who eagerly plunges his ramrod down the barrel. "What's wrong with them?" I whisper, though my ears are so shot I must have yelled, since Big Jim and Elmer both look at me.

Cyrus doesn't answer right away. He takes out a flask from his hip pocket, pops the cork, and takes a swig. Moonshine,

I'd guess, by the smell of it. The fumes almost choke me from three feet away.

He offers me the bottle. I shake my head. He shrugs and shoves the flask back into his pocket. He glances at Big Jim and Elmer, who have gone back to reloading.

"Their big brother could be down there," he whispers back.

"Brother? With the Union? But why isn't he up here with them?" I pause, then add, "With us?"

Cyrus shakes his head. "John Mark went up north to college a few years back. Now he says he don't believe in the secession. Don't think the South has the right to do it. He always was too durn stubborn for his own good."

Before he can go on, a Union drummer begins to beat and the Yankee soldiers step into Young's Branch.

Cyrus aims and fires.

"Just missed," he hisses.

Big Jim and Elmer raise their guns too, and fire. But their faces don't shine like Cyrus's when they pull the trigger.

Now two hundred yards in front of us, the line of Yankees rises up Henry Hill like an ocean tide, firing as they go. Bullets whistle above my head and plunk into the ground in front of me.

To my right, a big guy with shaggy sideburns raises his gun. If he was a reenactor, his gun wouldn't have a musket ball. It would just be full of powder so that it would *sound* like a real gun but not kill like one. And still he would aim well above the enemy's heads because, as Dad always preaches, "Even gunpowder firing from the barrel can hurt somebody."

Apparently, authenticity has its limits.

But this guy aims low, so he's sure at least to hit a Yankee in the leg or stomach. I wait for the blast, the shroud of smoke. Nothing happens. Suddenly the man falls forward face-first to the ground. The green grass under his head turns dark red.

I look back to Cyrus, but he doesn't even seem to notice what happened. Or he can't take time to notice because he's busy reloading. He raises his gun and fires. I look in the direction of his aim. One of the Yankee flags suddenly falls to the earth.

"Out durned spot!" Cyrus shouts.

The flag quickly rises again as another soldier grabs it up.

Angrily reloading, Cyrus glances at me. "Ain't you in this war? Ain't you going to shoot that gun?"

I realize I've been standing here like a total dork looking at all the action. I'm either going to have to start shooting or start running.

Running sounds a lot better.

If I start running the other way, maybe I can get far enough away before Cyrus sees me and can do anything about it. Not that he would. Guys like Cyrus will always be on the line of battle, never running for the rear.

I take a deep breath and start to tiptoe away, even though there's no way Cyrus can actually hear me from all the artillery blasts and gunfire. I take five steps. Ten. I've got my musket on my shoulder and it clangs against my bugle. I look over my shoulder. Cyrus still hasn't turned my way.

A few hundred yards ahead of me is the forest of cedars. If I can just make it to those, I'll be safe. Then all I'll need to do is figure out how this bugle will get me back home. I start to run. Faster. My musket clangs again and again off the bugle, but I don't care.

"Stonewall!" I hear Cyrus shout behind me. "Stonewall!"

Sorry, not this time, pal. With my head start, I know even I can beat him to the woods. And he's not going to leave his post anyway.

Running away from him makes me feel like a coward. Half my brain says I'm doing this so that I don't mess up history, but the other half is sneering at me and saying I am a big wuss and would probably be running away anyway.

A few more strides and the trees grow larger. My chest burns. The hundred-yard dash at school is one thing. What I've had to do today and what I'm doing now, loaded down with a bugle and musket, is freaking nuts.

But now I'm halfway there, only a couple hundred yards away. I can see the gaps in the trees, like they're opening up to welcome me inside. *Safe. Safe. Safe. Safe,* I gasp to myself to keep me going. I'm going to make it.

And suddenly they appear.

From out of the shadows of the trees step two solid ranks of at least a thousand Confederate soldiers, maybe two. Without a word, they all stop at once. I brake to a halt too. Most of the soldiers don't even seem to see me. They're looking at the fighting at my back. But some point at me and laugh. I look down at my light blue uniform and pathetic yellow neckerchief and feel like a complete dork trapped alone in this no-man's-land, like I'm in one of those screwy dodgeball games in PE where everybody has a ball but me.

To get out from under the gaze of thousands of eyes, I turn and see I'm much closer to the Confederate line than I thought I'd be. God, I am pathetic, I am so slow! But now I see that the Yankees have crested the hill and are almost to Mrs. Henry's house. It's not that I'm that slow. It's just that the Confederate line has been falling back with me.

A bullet whizzes by my head. Forget looking like a coward. I'm out of here. I spin around to make a dash for the trees . . . only to run face-first into the sweaty chest of this huge horse and hit the ground hard.

The sun is over the horse and rider, and the rider's face is in shadow. Another horse steps up to his right. I feel their breath and the stinky heat from their bodies.

"Running the wrong way, aren't you, son?" the rider says. His voice is low and harsh, and I jump to my feet quick.

The other horseback officer looks down on me. Unlike the soldiers, neither of them is laughing. Or even smiling.

"Sorry, sir," I gasp. "I just . . . I . . ."

And that's when I see his face.

He looks different. He's much younger and his beard is black and trimmed, not gray and shaggy. His blue eyes—lively and warm in his tent—are hard like rocks. And instead of a tie-dyed T-shirt, he has a stiff uniform. And both arms. But it's him! It has to be!

I should have guessed it earlier!

Relief floods through my body.

"Tom!" I say. "Man am I glad to see—"

His eyes cut to me now.

"What did you say, boy?" snaps the officer to his right.

"Sorry, sir," I say to the officer. "But, um, I know him. I mean, I know *you.*" I turn back to Tom, holding up the bugle as proof. "It's me."

Tom narrows his eyes at me even more.

"Me?" I whimper with a smile. "Stonewall?"

Tom sniffs and looks away from me to the advancing armies, while the other officer sneers, "Stonewall? *Stonewall?*"

He says the name in the same way I've always said it, like it was a huge black roach that I was about to stomp. With the possible exception of my father, Stonewall Jackson was the object of my greatest scorn and nastiest sarcasm. That he was actually shot and killed by his own men at the Battle of Chancellorsville has always been a bright spot in my Civil War studies. Only the belief that my ancestor Cyrus had turned chicken in the war's first fight seemed funnier.

Now I have to rethink this man too. Seeing him up on his horse, back straight and stiff, his long black beard waving in the wind as he looks calmly out over the battlefield, I can't think of him as *Stonewall.* I can't even think of him as Tom.

Only as General Jackson.

He glances at me one more time. "Mr. Stonewall, you'd better return to your regiment," he says, his voice as cold as his eyes. "Being shot is not the worst thing that could happen to you today."

My heart is pumping hard. I look into his face one more time, hoping for a wink or raised eyebrow or something to let me know he knows me.

But he turns away and I can see I'm not worth another ounce of his attention.

The Confederate line is now only fifty yards away. I can see Cyrus's red head through the dust and smoke. I'm not keen to the idea of getting back into the line, but General Jackson has made it clear I can't stay where I am. I start making my way back to Cyrus's side. I'm almost to him when I hear hoofbeats to my left. It's General Bee. He reins his horse to a stop between me and the Confederate line.

"Sound the fallback!" he yells over his shoulder.

I look up at him and realize he's talking to me.

"Sir?" I ask.

"Blow your bugle, *boy*, and sound the fallback!" he orders.

I unsling the bugle and put it to my lips. The Rebels are now less than twenty steps away. They bob up and down one at a time as they aim, fire, reload, aim, and fire again.

I breathe in deeply to sound the fallback. And stop. My gut flips and I gasp again.

I don't know the tune to fallback.

All I've ever had to play for the reenactments is *Charge!* I've learned a few other simple tunes, but never whatever *Fallback* is. Maybe it's the same as *Charge!* but the soldiers know which way they're supposed to go. Maybe this is also my ticket home. I close my eyes, take another breath, and blow.

I get six notes out before a hand smacks the bugle from my lips. I open my eyes to find General Bee, his face red, glaring at me from his horse. I guess *Charge!* wasn't right.

"Forget it, you fool," snarls General Bee. "I'll do it myself."

He turns back to the firing line and booms out the order.

"Fall back, men!" he cries. "Help has arrived!"

Looking at his men, General Bee draws his sword and points it toward me. Cyrus, Big Jim, and Elmer turn. Their faces are black from gun smoke. I see their white eyes flicker from Bee's sword to me.

"We are not alone!" Bee yells.

Now more eyes are on me. General Bee follows their confused looks.

"Not this idiot!" he shouts. I point over my shoulder and step behind Bee's horse, which uses that very moment to drop a load on my foot.

"Look, men!" Bee shouts. "Reinforcements! The Virginians!"

Now the soldiers see General Jackson, and the Yankees must see him too, because he's attracting a lot of enemy fire. You always shoot for the guy on a horse because horses carry only high-ranking officers. Bullets are whistling past his head. But he doesn't seem to care. He casually surveys the scene of battle as if he's watching the sunset. He turns to a young man beside him and issues an order. The young man scurries to the artillery pieces that have suddenly rolled out from the trees. At once, the cannons open fire above us and blast big holes in the Union line.

"Look, men!" General Bee shouts again, and I know the moment has come.

Up to today, General Jackson has been a military professor from Virginia who has gone by his given name, Thomas. But with General Bee's next sentence, General Jackson will get his immortal nickname—and I'll get mine.

"Look!" Bee shouts, and despite the chaos around me and

the childhood turmoil of being burdened with such a name, I feel this surge of excitement at getting to actually witness this event.

General Bee is about to say "There stands Jackson like a stone wall," and both Jackson and me will be stuck with that name forever.

"Soldiers of the South!" cries General Bee. "There stands Jackson like a . . . uh . . ."

Bee's grasping for the right words! This could be my chance! Maybe I can supply a better nickname for Jackson and a much better name for myself. Maybe Rock. Or Hammer. Or Lone Wolf. Or . . .

"Stone wall! Stone wall! Like a stone wall!" someone shouts.

Aw, man, who said that? The voice sounded familiar but I can't see who said it. But I can tell I just lost my chance, because Bee seems to love it. He points again with his sword. "There stands Jackson like a . . . stone wall!" he yells. "Rally behind the Virginians!" He spurs his horse and the entire line surges toward General Jackson.

I've missed my big chance. Now I am doomed to be Stonewall. The moment was in my hands and I let it slip away.

I trudge with the rest of the Confederates into General Jackson's line of men.

"I thought Stonewall had a nice ring to it, don't you think so, son?"

I look up. It's the familiar black hat. And the sunburn and goatee. And the way he licks the spittle away from his lips. This guy looks just like Senator Dupree, like maybe his great-grandfather or something.

He's patting other Confederates on the back, and gets smiles in return. But looking down I see what the other soldiers don't. His uniform is too nice, too clean, too starched. Like he hasn't been fighting at all. Like it's not even real.

And it hits me. This guy's wearing a reenactor's reproduction.

Just like mine.

This isn't Dupree's great-grandfather. This is Dupree. The real Dupree. Somehow, just like me, he's come back in time. Unlike me, he seems to be having a real good time.

"Yes, boys," I hear him say, "this war will be ours before the day is done."

CHAPTER SEVEN

ALL RIGHT, let's review.

It's 1861 and I'm in the middle of a freaking war zone with my great-great-great-great-uncle, who is not the wuss I grew up thinking but really some poetic kamikaze daredevil who's going to get me killed if I stay with him much longer. And now I've found myself face-to-face with a guy who makes the Ku Klux Klan look like the Boy Scouts.

Time to get out of here.

But here is the middle of a messy retreat, not nearly as orderly as when the reenactors do it. Maybe it's because real bullets aren't being fired at the reenactors. Men are pushing every which way and some don't seem to want to retreat. Some are still taking potshots at the Yankees. I wouldn't be surprised if Cyrus is one of them.

General Jackson's artillery is holding the Yankees back, but they are unloading on us with everything they've got. The cannon blasts have become a steady roar by the time we trudge the last few steps over a slight rise and into the ranks of General Jackson's brigade. There must be a couple of thousand men here, lying on the ground awaiting orders. Just beyond the men are some woods where litter bearers run in and out carrying the wounded and dead.

General Jackson has disappeared now, maybe gone to talk with other officers on the field. I don't take much time to look around for him. I throw myself to the ground behind a cedar (like that's really going to stop a cannonball) and bury my face in the grass, praying for the blasting to stop.

Each minute seems to last as long as a school day in spring. Shells explode over my head. Clods of earth and rocks shower down on my back. The shrieks and blasts of the artillery are occasionally answered by the screams of wounded soldiers.

Finally, the shelling slows down a little. Instead of a constant bombardment, several seconds pass between explosions. Both sides seem to be stopping for breath. Thank God! I can't take another minute of it.

Slowly, one by one, men rise to their elbows. Their faces are black or bloody or covered in mud. They look around at each other. Some crack smiles. Others roll onto their sides to reload their muskets. A few just sit there, not moving, staring at nothing. Some are heading to the rear, probably to get their wounds treated.

Maybe now I can escape. Behind me are two officers kneeling around a map, and no one else is paying attention to anything. I bet I could limp out of here, no problem, make it to the rear and keep on walking.

I slowly get to my hands and feet and start hobbling to the woods. I glance around for one last look at Cyrus, hoping I see him and at the same time hoping I don't see him.

I don't. But I do see Dupree. He's on his feet too, making his way to the two officers. He taps one on the shoulder. The officers turn and Dupree tries to show him some papers.

Well, whatever. This looks like a great time to slip away; all I have to do is pretend I'm wounded and follow the litter bearers out of here. Heck, I've done this in PE a million times.

Faking a limp, I make my way into the woods using my musket for a crutch. Once through the tree line, the sounds of gunfire behind me are replaced by the moans of wounded men. They lie on the ground in long rows in a small clearing. Most have blood somewhere on their clothes—their collars if a head wound, or their pants if they've been hit in the knee. One guy looks like he's wearing a lopsided shirt until I realize his right arm's been blown off.

All the more reason for me to hightail it out of here.

Women hurry from one soldier to the next, giving them water from canteens and wrapping rags around their wounds until they can be loaded onto a wagon and taken to the rear wherever they've set up the hospital.

I keep on going. If I can just get past all the people, somewhere by myself, I can ditch the gun and concentrate on this bugle once and for all. If I could just figure out how it worked. If only it had . . . instructions.

Oh my God!

It DOES have instructions. Tom/Stonewall Jackson/whoever gave them to me.

My hand flies to my pocket. Yes, still there.

Screw this limping act. I toss my musket in the grass and plop down beside the path to read the instructions. People are still racing past, but I should be home before anyone stops to ask me what I'm doing. I am totally out of here!

There are a couple sheets of clean paper wrapped around some antique, old-timey parchment kind of thing.

I can barely read the parchment, plus it's about to fall apart in my hands. So, I try the clean paper first. It's a letter from Tom. I frantically start reading. Good grief, how long is this thing?

> Young Stonewall,
>
> The Book has granted me several years' time to write this letter, but I feel you will have only a few minutes to read it, so I will come directly to the point.

You call this directly? I need some help here, dude!

> By now you must realize that you are indeed in 1861 at the real Battle of Bull Run.

No duh!

> And you may have even run into me already. I regret that I wasn't more friendly to you . . .

More friendly? You weren't any friendly!

> . . . but I had no way of knowing your importance to me and to the proper course of history.

Importance? I'd really rather not be important if you don't mind. I'd much rather know how to get the heck out of here.

> You may be wondering why I've placed such a burden on you, but you must understand that I did not choose you. That you simply are the person who

will have attempted these things. And I place all
my faith and hope in your success. I know that you
believe, as I do, that there are things in the present
worth fighting for in the past.

Fighting in the past for the present? What? Did I mention
that I'd rather get the heck out of here?

Let me explain what I know of the situation,
or at least what I think will happen. I believe that
another time traveler, the Weapon Wielder, is in
1861 with you now and I am almost certain that it is
Senator Dupree.

Well, Tom got that one right. But what's this Weapon
Wielder business? Everybody here wields a weapon.

He's a hateful, evil man and, if he has the Weapon,
he's a very dangerous man. I think he may have killed
to get the Weapon and he'll very likely kill you if
you try to interfere with him.

I have a really bad feeling about what the next sentence is
going to say. I'm really worried it will say, "but interfere you
must." I flip the page over and keep reading . . .

But interfere you must! I fear he plans to use the
Weapon to alter the course of history. To help the
South win the war. Yes, the South, the very side I
fought for, but which I now know to have been very
much in the wrong. Now I understand the extraordi-
nary injustice of slavery and the countless contribu-
tions that African Americans as a free people have
made to . . .

Well, it's good to know he's seen the light, but right now

66

I need some actual help. I skim ahead looking for something about the bugle . . .

> Like your bugle, which is known as the Instrument, the Weapon allows Dupree, or whoever might possess it, to travel into and out of the past. These two items are devices called Tempests, used for making changes in the time stream. Where they came from I cannot say. Whether science or magic I cannot say. Most of what I know comes from the Instructions, which I hereby pass on to you. It may be difficult for you to understand them at first.

I unfold the old-timey-looking paper. These are supposed to be instructions?

Difficult to understand? Try impossible! I mean, what the heck? Lines and hammers and jibber jabber all over a raggedy piece of paper. Good God, does that say Ben Franklin? How did he get mixed up in all this? What's the deal with his handwriting? Oh here's a piece I can read:

> The Instrument, the weakest of the Tempests . . .

Oh great. That's just freaking great! How did I get the weakest one?

> The Instrument, the weakest of the Tempests, and the Weapon will be useful in traveling to the past, but note that they cannot take one into his own future nor can they be used to bring someone forward from the past since that person would be traveling into their own future though it be only the user's present.

Instructions for the use of the

Five Tempests Devices

for temporal and spatial adjustments.

Note: Alexander who briefly possessed the crown never used it apparently fearful of some great cost exacted on the user. He believed that Ullyses had used the crown and his years of wandering and suffering were a result.

Note: The crown is the only template to allow travel to both one's past and future

Spacial

Parabola of — the BOOK

Allowing for the exploration of future and accumulation of all knowledge gained during elapsed time free and instant movement on the spacial axis, but only forward movement on temporal axis.

Note: Even another tempest cannot return book to past. It moves forward only.

Having had opportunity to try either the Book or the Instrument I chose this book having no reason or wish to revisit the past I sprang forward in an instant through a full fortnight saving exhausted and dizzy with new found knowledge and understanding. It was with regret that I gave this book back to N.B.

The Instruments and the Weapon

Allowing for movement backwards along the temporal axis.

Note: The Instrument is the weakest of the tempests, and the Weapon will be useful in traveling to the past, but note that they cannot take one into his own future nor can they be used to bring someone forward from the past since that person would be traveling into their own future though it be only the user's present.

Note: Mind Ye well that the ...strument can ...ly carry the user ...tween certain time ...tures, severely limiting ...usefulness when ...pared with the weapon. ...thout proper precautions the ...trument carrier may ...himself stranded in time ...ting the next temporal juncture

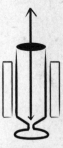

Span of the | Great HAMMER

allowing multiple movements of multitudes on the spatial axis, not affecting and regardless of the temporal.

Note: Ptolemy suggested Hammer was true means of Hannibals passage through the Alps. But Tycho Brache used the Instrument to disprove this.

Translated and transcribed
this day, July 10, 1787,
by my hand
Benj. Franklin

Fine, fine. I don't need to carry anyone forward, I just need to get my own butt forward before I get shot in it like Cyrus. Why don't these instructions explain why this piece of crap bugle isn't working anymore? Oh wait . . .

> Mind ye well that the Instrument can only carry the user between certain time junctures, severely limiting its usefulness when compared with the Weapon. Without proper precautions, the Instrument Carrier may find himself stranded in time a'waiting the next time juncture.

Well, these instructions suck. Here's what I've learned so far:

a) Dupree, an evil history-changing wacko has his own time bazooka.

b) Me, a wimp, has his very own wussy magic bugle.

c) I'm stuck here until the next time juncture, whatever or whenever that is.

d) These instructions suck.

I've about given up, but I look back over Tom's letter in case I missed something useful.

> Yes, Stonewall, I fear for history itself. I fear for every gain our nation has made since the Civil War. I fear that Dupree will craft a new history, one where the slaves are never freed, where the Union is dissolved, where what's left of the United States is not powerful enough to stop Hitler. Where Martin Luther King never . . .

Holy crap! How exactly did I get mixed up in all this again? How does Tom expect me to do anything about all this? Is he not aware that I'm just a loser who can't even win at a Play-Station game without a cheat code?

What in the name of all that's holy am I going to do?

"Stonewall?" I hear a girl's voice call out.

It's so impossible that it must be my imagination. But I turn around anyway and there she is.

"Oh my God, I'm so glad to see you," Ash says at the same time that I say, "What are you doing here?"

"This is real, right?" she asks. "We're really here in the . . ." She looks around and whispers, " . . . the real Civil War."

Her curly brown hair is all messed up and it's tough to tell what's dirt and what's freckles on her face. But her eyes are as big and beautiful as ever—maybe even more beautiful after all the terrible stuff I've seen today.

I reach out to hug her . . . and see that she's got blood on her dress.

"You've been shot!" I almost scream.

She looks down. "No, no, no. I've just been treating the wounded."

"Really? You know how?"

She shrugs. "Nursing's my job at the reenactments."

"Yeah, but this . . ." I say.

She gives me a brave grin. "Yeah, there's the blood and all. But it's no different than you knowing how to blow that bugle or fire that gun."

That hurts. At least she's half right.

We take a few steps away from the path, which is starting to get busy with men running back and forth. Actually, they're running forth and get carried back, if you know what I mean.

"So do you know how to get back?" I ask.

"I was hoping you did."

"No clue. All I've got are a wussy magic bugle and Ben Franklin's chicken scratch instructions," I say, showing her the aforementioned chicken scratching. But I can tell I'm just confusing her.

So I tell her what happened to me as quick as I can, and when I'm finished she gives me her story.

Apparently after she left me at the reenactment, she was trying to catch up with her father to get the keys to his pickup because she'd left her nurse's bag inside.

"But I didn't mind because I wanted to check up on Dad anyway since he acted awfully funny this morning. He actually gave me a hug good-bye before 'going off to battle,' as he put it."

But when Ash had just about caught up to him, the battle started. Everybody started running, except her father. He bent down and pulled out a tiny gun from an ankle holster. That's right, a tiny gun. A Weapon.

Ash called him, but there was so much noise he couldn't hear. She reached out and grabbed his sleeve, and that's when he fired the gun in the air.

Suddenly, she was here. And so was he.

Yep, Tom was right, I realize; Dupree's tiny gun must be the Weapon Tempest thing. At least it's not a time bazooka like I was worried about.

"Couldn't your father have taken you back?" I ask.

"I guess, if he wasn't busy acting like a lunatic." It looks like she's starting to cry, but I can't tell if they're regular tears or mad tears. Probably both.

"When I finally got his attention, I tried to ask him what was going on, but he was furious. He was like, 'What are you doing here!' Soldiers were rushing all around us and bumping into us and I was terrified and he was just screaming at me. 'Can't you take me back,' I begged him, but he said he didn't have time. He told me to run and hide in the rear and he would try to look for me later, like I was absolutely nothing."

I hardly even know what to say. The best I can do is "Geez." But then I have an idea.

"Let me try the bugle," I say. "Maybe it'll take us home. Then we can figure things out . . ."

I reach out and take her hand. I raise the bugle—cold and clammy—and give a toot. Nothing at all happens.

"I told you it was lame," I say. "I guess this isn't one of Ben Franklin's time junctures. Well, we probably shouldn't go home without your dad anyway."

"He can probably take care of himself."

"That's not exactly what I mean," I say. "I'm kind of supposed to stop him."

"Stop him from what?"

"Well . . ." I wish I had time to think of a better way to explain this.

"You know how your father wishes the South had won? Well . . ."

I hand her Tom's letter, pointing to the bit about changing

history and the slaves and Hitler and all that. I try to cover up the part about him killing someone.

I expect her to say, "No, my dad would never do all that," which is what I would say.

"Last night, I was telling you how crazy he is," she says quietly, "but you don't know half of it. He thinks that if the South had won, everything would be perfect for him and people like him. He wouldn't have had all his problems . . . wouldn't have gone to jail . . . would be some kind of powerful man! And the rest of the country would be just the way he wants it too. No rap music, no immigrants, no 'weirdos.' Just him and his good old boys running the show."

She looks up at me. "But even if he wants to change all that, how can he? He's just a reenactor, not a real soldier."

"It could be pretty easy, actually," I said. "Did you ever see *Back to the Future*? I mean, you can mess up the past without even meaning to. Just think what your father could do on purpose! Especially since he knows so much about the war. He could shoot an important Yankee or block one of the bridges or . . . "

My mind flashes back to what I saw Dupree doing earlier. " . . . or he could just tell a couple of officers what the Yankees are planning to do next. And that's exactly what he was doing when I saw him. Oh crap. It may already be too late."

"But can't we undo the things he's doing?" asked Ash. "Can't we try to keep history the same?"

I guess this is the time for me to say something heroic. But I've never said anything heroic before. I try to remember that thing Tom wrote about fighting in the future for the past or something, but I can't keep it all straight anymore.

So I give sort of a heroic sigh.

"Uhhhhhhhh. Yeah, I guess that's why Tom sent me back here."

"And I can help too," she says.

She grabs my arm and pulls me back toward the battle.

"C'mon, let's go back and try to see what he's up to."

Whoa! She's starting to sound a little like Cyrus. Go back? To the battlefield? I spent the whole morning trying to get out!

I'd like to tell her that I prefer not to be bayoneted, shot, or crapped on by any more famous horses.

But she's got her hand on my arm and I think she could lead me anywhere. Oh yeah, plus it's a noble cause too. But mostly I think it's her hand on my arm.

CHAPTER EIGHT

WE STOP at the edge of the woods and look out over the battlefield. There's a lull in the battle, but of course we know that won't last long. From here we mostly see the rear of the Confederate lines as soldiers move about, reloading, regrouping, and trying to dodge the occasional artillery shell.

I can see Cyrus. I think I can see Big Jim and Elmer there too. It's hard to tell from this far away and with so many people in the way.

I point out Cyrus to Ash and tell her a little about what he and I have been through.

"Great," she says, "maybe he'll be able to help us."

"Well, except for the fact that he's crazy and a Confederate too," I say.

"Perfect," she says. "He may actually be the best thing we've got going for us."

We keep looking and finally Ash spots her father. It looks like he's giving another one of his speeches, not that far from where Cyrus is.

"He seems to be staying clear of the front line," I say. "He doesn't want to get shot either, obviously. It doesn't look like he's actually done much yet."

"Maybe we can just find out what he's up to and screw it up," says Ash.

Finally! Something I'm good at. Screwing stuff up. Maybe there is hope after all.

"But," she adds, "we can't do much from back here."

So we make a plan. It's the dumbest plan I've ever heard of in my life. The part that's most dumb is the part where I go back to find Cyrus, so he and I can try to get involved in whatever Dupree is doing and mess it up. Meanwhile, Ash is going to hang around in the rear near her father to try to find out what he's up to by pretending to do nurse-type stuff.

Yeah, I know, I told you it was dumb. But what else were we going to do?

I linger for a minute hoping there's going to be a big kiss when we separate, but she only gives me a big hug, which is nice too.

"Don't do anything crazy," she says.

But I'm already doing something crazy. I'm actually going back to the battlefield to get shot at some more. It was a lot easier to talk about saving the world when we weren't actually looking at the battle. There are just so many people and they seem to fall over dead almost at random.

I promise myself that I'm going to be careful, keep my head down, and not let Cyrus get me killed.

I step carefully out of the woods, back into the shriek of

artillery shells and gunfire. Thankfully, it's still off and on, nothing as bad as earlier. I take a quick look down the line but I can't see Cyrus's red head anymore. I keep low and fall down alongside the other soldiers behind the rise.

The artillery suddenly stops completely. There doesn't even seem to be any gunfire either. We're not shooting at them and they aren't shooting at us. That will change soon, but for now it's actually quiet.

I push myself up to my knees to look around. Still no Cyrus. This whole thing about stopping Dupree seems impossible. But if I have to try, I need to have Cyrus with me. I sure can't do this myself, and I'm starting to get the feeling that Cyrus can do anything. Except stop talking or show concern for his personal safety. Or mine.

I don't want to, but if I'm going to find him, I'm going to have to get up and start going forward again. I get to my feet and take three steps before I realize I've left my musket. I can't show up next to Cyrus with only my bugle. I go back and grab it and start walking down the line. I stay low to the ground just in case some Yankee sharpshooter wants to get lucky.

Stretched out all along the ground are the other soldiers— or I guess I should say the *real* soldiers, since I haven't even fired a shot yet. They're older than me, but not by much. Some like Big Jim and Elmer, who I assume are with Cyrus, are barefoot and wear overalls. Only the officers wear uniforms, and most of theirs, like General Jackson's, are the blue ones they have from their time in the U.S. Army before the South seceded. No one has the gray Confederate uniforms yet. No one thinks the war is going to last long enough for the South to have time to make uniforms.

You'll have plenty of time, guys. Too much time.

I also notice that each soldier also has a different kind of gun. That's probably because each man has to arm himself to fight. The North has all the factories that make the guns, and they certainly aren't going to sell to the South. So some men have old muskets while a few have the new Enfield rifles that fire lead minié balls, which look like modern bullets.

When you read about this stuff in the history books, it just seems like a long boring list of guns. But now I can see that it makes a heck of a lot of difference whether you've got the fancy new rifle or if you're stuck with your granddaddy's flintlock. It probably means the difference between shooting a Yankee and getting shot by a Yankee.

As I make my way down the line trying to spot Cyrus, I realize that most all the men share one thing—they all seem anxious. Not scared, just concerned. Their faces aren't as happy as they were when I first appeared on the field. They've seen too much suffering already today. They are volunteers. Most of them, I bet, had visions when they enlisted of doing heroic things in battle. But I wonder how many had thought about what really happens in war, that you might really get shot, get killed. I don't think my father and his reenactors think too much about this part of a Civil War soldier's life. How can you and still want to reenact it?

More and more wounded Confederates crawl into our line from the direction of Mrs. Henry's house, which now has Union artillery planted on either side and a sea of Yankees swirling all around. A few Confederates trickle in from the woods behind us, but the numbers on our side don't seem nearly as great as those preparing to come at us.

"Don't worry!" I want to tell the guys on the ground as I pass. "I know it looks bad right now, but you're going to win!"

But some may not. Some are going to die or lose a leg or an eye, and they probably won't feel like they've won anything. And Cyrus still has to get his wound. God, I hope that hasn't already happened! I need him now in one piece, not laid up with his butt in a sling.

But he's fine. I spot him crouching on the ground among some other guys. The Union artillery has picked back up and most of the soldiers bury their faces in their arms. But not Cyrus. And not Big Jim and Elmer, whose faces are black from gunpowder but I still recognize them lying on either side of him.

Cyrus has just finished loading his musket and is pulling back the hammer.

"Cyrus," I call out.

He doesn't seem to hear me, but sights his musket at something close to the Henry House. I plop down beside him just as he pulls the trigger.

"Durn!" he snaps at me. "You made me miss!"

I doubt this, considering the house is like five football fields away. He turns to look at me. "Oh," he says, his eyes narrowing at me. "It's you. I thought you had snuck off."

He turns his back to me to reload his gun. I don't need to ask him why he's mad at me. I know. I ran. While he and Big

Jim and Elmer and all the other Confederates stood in line, firing their guns and getting fired on, I ran. In his eyes, I'm a coward. I deserve the same sarcasm I've always dished out at reenactments. As I watch Cyrus ram another ball into his musket, shame hits me doubly hard—at my wrongful treatment of him in the past, and his rightful treatment of me today.

I just want a chance to explain myself.

"Cyrus, I'm sorry," I say to his back. "I'm sorry I ran, but I don't belong here. I'm not supposed to be here."

He rolls onto his stomach and takes aim with his gun. For the first time today, he has nothing to say to me. But Big Jim does.

"Don't nobody belong here," he says. "But here's where we're at."

He fires. For a moment, we're shrouded in gunpowder smoke. The smell burns my nostrils and tears come to my eyes for the hundredth time today.

"I need you to listen to me."

Cyrus has pulled out his flask again and takes a drink. He doesn't offer the bottle to me this time.

"Shoot," he says.

I take a deep breath and prepare to let it all come out at once.

"It's not a coincidence we have the same last name. I am your—"

A massive eruption cuts me off. Dirt and rock and blood pepper our bodies, our faces. We look up and as the cloud of smoke lifts, we can see in front of us to our right a few men sprawled in a pit where an artillery shell has just burst. They are, or were, Confederates falling back from Henry House to our line. They had almost made it when the shell hit.

They all look dead, a pile of twisted arms and legs. Suddenly a hand twitches. The hand seizes a leg and tosses the limb aside. Now we can see the man attached to the hand. He lurches upright, blood matted in his blond beard, and starts hobbling toward us. One of his legs looks like it's been run over. He makes it a few feet and collapses, a sitting duck in the no-man's-land between us and the Yankees.

A bullet whizzes over my head and I duck down. When I open my eyes again, Cyrus is gone. I glance behind me. Of course he's nowhere in sight there.

"Cyrus!" I hear Big Jim scream. I look at the big man. His eyes, wide in his blackened face, stare toward the Yankee line.

I follow his gaze.

"Oh, God."

Cyrus has gone back over the rise shielding us from Yankees. He's kneeling by the wounded man in clear sight of enemy fire.

Big Jim makes a move to help, but just as quick Elmer grabs him by the legs.

"Get off me!" Big Jim hollers. He struggles against his brother, even smacks Elmer across the face with the back of his hand. But Elmer squeezes tighter. His face is white, clenched.

"I ain't losing you too," Elmer groans. "Not for something that pointless."

It's the first thing I've heard him say today, but it does the trick. Big Jim stops fighting and lies still.

I turn back to Cyrus, who grabs the wounded man's wrist and pulls his arm around over his neck. Getting his feet beneath him, Cyrus heaves the man to his back and stands. Cyrus's face turns scarlet as he staggers under the man's weight.

He starts running toward our line. Suddenly, I hear the *splat* of a bullet hitting flesh. Cyrus tumbles forward.

"No!"

But just as quickly Cyrus is back on his feet. The bullet apparently hit the other man in the back. Another few feet and the two of them collapse beside me.

"Are you crazy?!" I yell at him.

Cyrus lies on the ground for a moment gasping for air. It takes just a glance at the wounded man he's carried back to tell that he's dead.

"Are you crazy?!" I yell again.

Cyrus looks blankly at me. "What are you talking about?"

"He's dead!" I scream.

"I didn't know that," he replies, reaching for his gun.

"You could have been killed!"

Cyrus wrinkles his forehead. "Well . . . yeah."

And suddenly, like some thick fog has lifted from the earth, all is clear and peaceful. The sun shines warmly across the fields, the sky blazes blue. It might actually be a nice afternoon, if you could ignore the thousands of Yankees taking their time to reorganize not half a mile from where we lie in a line of battle. I know from the history books that the Union commander, General McDowell, has simply broken off the fight for an hour or so to get his men in a solid line to charge us again. Big mistake, McDowell!

I turn back to Cyrus, who is clutching his gun to his chest and trying to reload it.

"Why do you do that?" I ask.

"What?"

"Why do you have to be so . . . so . . . ." I want to find just the right word that won't offend him but still show my concern. I rule out *stupid, idiotic, nuts, gonzo,* and *freaky.*

"Why do you have to be so gallant?"

Cyrus stops loading and looks at me. "Gallant . . . gallant . . . I like that. More poetic than *brave* or something like that. Reminds me of Galahad . . . Sir Galahad searching for the Holy Grail and a way to redeem the Round Table. That'd make a good story too. Set today of course . . . with a guy searching for the meaning of life who goes off to battle and . . ."

He goes on, the stress on his face fading away. Big Jim and Elmer, who were hovering over him, shake their heads and roll back to their place in line.

Even though I want to stay angry, I can't stop myself from smiling.

He finally pauses the story in his mind and I jump in.

"I'm glad you like gallant, but I don't understand why you're willing to get yourself killed."

He rams the ball into his gun, lays his head back, and stares into the sky.

"It's just in my nature," he says.

I look at the dead soldier lying a few feet from us. That could have been Cyrus. And I remember: That will be Cyrus.

He's *supposed* to get shot. Today. At Bull Run. And he's *supposed* to die. That's my family's heritage.

Of course, I've learned that my heritage isn't as crappy as I thought. He's obviously going to get wounded from some act of heroism—and not cowardice as I've thought for all my life. That should make me pleased, if nothing else.

Instead it makes me sad. And angry.

Now I know why I got so angry seeing him go over that hill. Whatever Dupree's plans, that's one part of history that I don't want to happen.

I don't want Cyrus to die. I want him to live.

"I was born in Big Lick, Virginia, on a bend in the Roanoke River that's about the prettiest place on earth."

For a second, I wonder if Cyrus is daydreaming. Lying on his back and looking up at the sky, Cyrus seems like he's talking more to himself than to me. His voice is faraway, like he's in shock from a wound. I quickly scan his body for blood. I almost ask him to roll over so I can look at his butt, but given my performance so far today, I don't think he'd react too well.

He turns his head to me. His eyes are clear and look right into mine. He's not hurt. He just feels like talking. Maybe it's starting to sink in that he almost got himself killed. I see Big Jim give Elmer a look and the two of them go off to get more ammunition.

But I'm more than happy to listen. Anything to steer the conversation away from me.

"I grew up on a farm with my daddy and brother Joshua.

Joshua was about ten years older than me and I sometimes thought of him more like an uncle than my big brother. He was tall and real friendly with bushy blond hair and a toothy smile, unlike my daddy, who was built low and gnarled like a scrub bush."

Cyrus pauses. He wrinkles his forehead and mutters, "Like a scrub bush . . . that's pretty good too. Lordy, I'm getting all kinds of inspiration on this here field. Whether I'm going to be able to remember it all to write down is another thing."

He shrugs. "Anyway, Momma died when I was born, so it was just the three of us working the land. Sometimes I'd hike the ridge that rose up across the river and stand on this high rock outcropping and pretend I was seeing the end of the world. 'Course it wasn't the end of the world, just more and more of those blue mountains stretching off into forever. And seeing that that was all to the world made me feel just fine living on the banks of the Roanoke River in Big Lick, Virginia.

"But it never seemed to Joshua's liking. He was always coming up with these get-rich ideas. Like when I was about eleven years old, he marched into the house smacking his fist into his palm. It was a Sunday afternoon and Daddy was smoking his pipe by the fireplace and Joshua says, 'Daddy, Cyrus, it's time to seek our fortune.' This was what he always said before landing one of his tall ones on us."

If I understand my family tree right, Joshua was actually my great-great-great-grandfather. Or something like that.

Hearing Cyrus talk about Joshua, I can't help but think ADD has been in the family a long, long time. "Maybe that's where you got it from," I murmur, a bit too loud.

"Got what?" Cyrus says.

"Oh . . . uh, telling stories," I say.

Cyrus stares at me and suddenly this smile bursts on his face. "I'd never thought of that."

"So what was his fortune?"

Cyrus leans back. "He says in this real grand sort of way, 'I've been surveying our estate and the holdings of our esteemed neighbors and I've discovered that what our community needs is a mill.' Now Daddy takes the pipe from his mouth and says, 'What's wrong with the one we've got in Tinker?' Joshua says, 'Tinker may be just a half-day's journey for us, but plenty of folks have to travel even further and they're going right by us to get there.'"

A half-day's journey? In a wagon down some bumpy dirt road? Just to get flour made? Sounds like reason enough for me to build anything. Thank God for Food Lion.

Cyrus continues. "Seeing that Daddy had started smoking again, Joshua turned his attention to me. As always, his scheming hooked my interest. 'I still say we need a mill!' he declared. 'And I'm going to build it!' And so he did. He bought an acre of land from Daddy and on that one acre built his mill right on the river. Seemed like right away he was making money hand over fist. First off he would grind anybody's crop. Tinker wouldn't deal with the handful of free colored families who live in the county. But Joshua

87

would. 'Their money's the same color as a white man's,' he'd say."

Free blacks? In Virginia? And Joshua treated them the same as whites? I look hard at Cyrus to see if he's joking. I always think of all blacks in the South as slaves and all whites as slave-owners, but it was a lot more complicated than that. Joshua seems like one of the complicated parts.

Cyrus is still gazing at the sky and talking away.

"Well, after about three years, Joshua comes marching into the house again on a Sunday and says, 'Gentlemen, it's time to seek our fame and fortune.' Daddy says, 'Ain't you got enough fortune already?' Joshua says, 'No such thing as enough.' He hooked his thumbs into the lapels of his coat. 'You heard of a place called Harpers Ferry?' If Daddy had, he didn't let on. Joshua knew I hadn't, so he began to tell me how Harpers Ferry is a town way far away from us. Hundreds of miles. To get there you go down the Shenandoah Valley along a road that ain't made of dirt but is actually paved with stones! And in Harpers Ferry there are hotels with fancy restaurants and stores that sell candy canes and boots and silver watches and knives. And wouldn't you know it but Harpers Ferry has got not one, but two rivers flowing by, and each one could swallow twenty Roanoke Rivers. And do you know what they make in Harpers Ferry? Guns. Lots of guns. They got whole big factories that make guns for the U.S. government. And do you know what runs them factories? You got it. Mills. Big huge ones that you could fit ten of Joshua's inside. And do you know what runs the mills? Men, that's who. Men who get paid fifty cents a day. Fifty cents! Why, a man would make more there in a week than he would two months in Big Lick. A man could be rich!"

Whoopee! Fifty cents! I guess that was a lot back then . . . I mean, now. But there's something about Cyrus's story that sounds familiar. Something about Harpers Ferry that I'm supposed to know but can't remember. One of my dad's stories that I ignored.

Cyrus says, "Daddy didn't understand why getting rich was so important to Joshua. Said all the fortune he ever wanted was right at home. I don't think Joshua really cared about the money either. He just wanted more to life, so a month later he left. After he was gone, my view of the world suddenly seemed pretty small. I'd always figured everything I ever needed was on that farm, but now I knew there was a whole lot more out there. I just didn't know if I'd ever get the chance to see it. Or if I had the guts to go see it for myself."

The words just pop out of my mouth. "I can't imagine you not having guts for anything."

I feel my face go red at sounding so gushy. Cyrus looks embarrassed too, but pleased at the same time. It takes him a few seconds to continue with his story.

"What I also didn't know then was that I'd never see Joshua again. We got a package from him a couple of months after he left. Inside was this book of Shakespeare plays and these knives . . ." Cyrus pats the hilts on his hips. "One for me and one for Daddy, though Daddy sent his with me when I joined up. Joshua wrote about how big and busy Harpers Ferry was.

How the streets were all paved and trains come and go just about every hour. He also told us about a woman he met, Miss Jenny Richmond, and that they were getting married and he looked forward to us meeting his bride.

"But the next letter we got from Harpers Ferry was in a different handwriting. Envelope said it was from Mrs. Joshua Hinkleman. Daddy opened it and started reading it aloud to me, but he stopped after the first sentence. He kept reading it quiet. Halfway through, he started crying. I'd never seen him do that before. When he finished, he slumped into his rocking chair. All he said was, 'Joshua is dead.' Joshua's wife didn't have many facts in her letter. What she said was there was this crazy white man named John Brown—an abolitionist, she called him—who rounded up a bunch of slaves and went to Harpers Ferry and took over one of the gun arsenals. They killed a bunch of folks. Joshua and some others tried to stop them and Joshua was shot and died the next day."

"Whoa!" I shout. "John Brown? *The* John Brown? John Brown killed Joshua?"

Cyrus looks at me strange and slowly nods. He says something that I don't hear because my heart is pumping so hard in my head.

John Brown killed Cyrus's brother, my great-great-great-grandfather! Now I remember why Harpers Ferry is important—John Brown's raid in 1859 caused even more friction between the North and South and led to the South's decision to secede. And the Civil War to start.

But if all this is true, how the heck was I born?

I ask Cyrus if there was a baby and he says, "Yep, a baby without a father."

I barely hear what Cyrus says next. "So when Virginia declared, I told Daddy I was going to join up with the army. He didn't try to talk me out of it, but he wouldn't come with me. Said it would end up being a rich man's war but a poor man's fight. He said the plantation men with all the money and slaves were the only ones who wanted to secede, but they weren't the ones who'd do the fighting. But the way I see it, the North is full of men like John Brown. Men who killed my brother and now want to come down here and tell us how to live. Daddy may be right about the plantation men, but some things are worth fighting for. Like family and home."

"But John Brown was trying to free slaves," I say, more to myself. "I mean, that's what the war was all about."

I look up at Cyrus. He's got a scowl on his face and he says real low, "Joshua didn't have no durn slaves. Daddy and me don't have no durn slaves. This ain't about the slaves. This is about us being free."

"Oh I know, I know," I say, trying quick to calm him down. "I'm sorry. I just . . . well . . . I didn't know so many Southerners didn't feel free. Is that really why you're fighting? Freedom?"

It takes Cyrus a second to cool off. Finally, he says, "Mostly . . . well, partly . . ."

He looks down our line to the left and away to the west.

91

I look too. Way in the distance, over all the soldiers and horses and wagon trains and artillery, the mountains are just visible.

"Partly it's also about those blue mountains," he says. "Like I said, after Joshua left Big Lick, I got to wondering where those mountains lead . . . what's at the end of them . . . and beyond. I figured if there was ever a chance to see the world . . . experience it, if you know what I mean . . . really have an adventure, then this was it. So I signed up to join, and Big Jim and Elmer signed up too, though I think they did it in part to keep an eye out for me. And here we are."

CHAPTER NINE

EVERYTHING'S CALM on the battlefield, but I'm blown away by Cyrus's story. I thought I had this Civil War stuff down cold. The South just wanted to keep slavery alive and my ancestors were a bunch of wussies too afraid to fight.

"But why are you so reckless?" I ask again.

"You mean gallant, don't you?" he asks. I thought I'd made him mad, but he looks over at me with a wild grin.

The shriek of a cannonball cuts through the quiet. It doesn't land close, but it looks like the fighting is starting back up again. I just have a minute or two to make Cyrus understand what is really going on here. I take a deep breath again and let the words tumble out.

"Cyrus, it's not a coincidence that we have the same last name. We really are related. We're kin. Only I'm from, like, a hundred and fifty years in the future. Somehow I've come back in time. I think it has to do with this bugle."

I hold the bugle out to him. "Anyway, sometime today you're supposed to get shot in the butt. But that's not the important part. Well, it is important . . . *you'll* think it's important and I bet it'll hurt a lot . . . but that's not why I'm telling you all . . . though you really need to stop doing the stuff that you're doing so you won't get shot. But the real reason I'm telling you all this is because there's another guy who's come back in time with me and he's trying to . . ."

My voice trails off. He's not listening to me. He's looking at my bugle, which still gleams like new. Cyrus eyes it a moment and looks up at me real slow and says, "Okay, let's see it do some magic."

"Well . . . uh . . . it won't work right now," I say. "I've got to wait for . . . uh . . . a temporal juncture."

"Stonewall," he begins, "maybe you really *should* head to the rear. I think you've got battle fever. I mean, I know I'm weird sometimes, but your actions show much like to madness: pray heaven your—"

Before Cyrus can finish, a feeble cheer goes up from the men lying around us. We turn and see General Jackson on his horse emerging from the woods and back into our ranks. With him are two other officers—the two officers that Dupree has been talking to! They seem to be plotting strategy, but before they're within earshot, they salute General Jackson and gallop away.

But no one watches them go. All eyes are on General Jackson as he canters by. He looks beyond us to the line of Union soldiers stretching from either side of Mrs. Henry's house. Their line seems to lengthen every minute as more reinforcements extend it.

As if he's solved a puzzle, General Jackson nods and turns his attention to us. He scans every soldier in his sight. His eyes hit mine and a chill rushes over me. With his fierce blue eyes and wild black beard, he's so scary I can't believe he's somehow going to become the hippy dude I met last night.

He wheels his horse around.

"Men!" he cries. "The fate of our new nation hangs on this hill! If we lose this hill, we lose our country! If we hold it, we gain our freedom!"

He pauses and the field is silent, as if the Yankees also wait for his words.

"What will it be?" General Jackson at last declares.

"Freedom!" the soldiers yell. Their red, grimy faces are twisted in pain or pleasure, I can't tell which as I study them. Everyone, that is, except Senator Dupree. I spy his black-hatted self down the line, stroking his goatee and nodding at the manic men on either side of him.

Now General Jackson nods too. "Then let us defend it."

As if the Yankees have heard all they want, a voice erupts from across the field.

"Charge!"

A drum beats, a bugle blows, and the Union line begins its advance. Behind them, their artillery continues blasting shells over their heads and into our line.

At once, orders from General Jackson's officers ripple down the army. The men around us begin to pepper the Yankees with cannon and musket shot. This checks their momentum, but they don't retreat. They don't duck for cover or hide behind trees either, while they shoot. They simply stand in line and open fire on our line, which is also standing, unprotected, and firing at them.

I've seen reenactors do this before—stand in formation as they aim their muskets at the reenacted enemy, fire, reload, aim, and fire again.

But this . . . good God! How do they just stand there, taking turns being the hunter and hunted? These men may be untrained, but the bullets whizzing by their heads might as well be flies. I try to shield myself behind this beast of a dude, his shoulders as wide as a refrigerator. Cyrus is to his right. He's reloading and looks over his shoulder at me. I act like I'm reloading too, even though I haven't even fired a shot yet. He just shakes his head at me, takes aim, and fires again.

I know who the winner will be, but it doesn't seem obvious from where I'm standing. Peeking around the refrigerator's side, I see the Union line growing longer on either end. I look to my left, to the end of our line. The Yankees have more men there. It's only a matter of time before they surround us.

Suddenly I see the familiar dark goatee and big hat of General Bee. On his horse, he motions with his sword for his brigade to get in a battle line. He scans the men on both sides of him and raises his sword. The odds are long, but he is going to attack the Yankees before they get the chance to encircle us.

I can't hear his voice over the chaos of the battle, but as his sword drops the troops charge.

"Rally, men!" someone close to me shouts. It's a Confederate officer, a tall, thin guy with a pale face and circles around his eyes. I recognize him as one of the officers who Dupree was talking to. Sure enough, in a flash Dupree is at his side, his eyes darting from the soldiers who are gathering around the officer to a piece of paper in his hand. I work my way next to Dupree and see him look from the paper to a hill about a hundred yards away to our left. I crane my neck to snatch a peek at the paper. Just as quick, Dupree turns back and catches me looking. I glance away, but still feel his eyes burning a hole in the top of my head as I hear him fold up the paper and tuck it away.

But I saw all I needed to see. The paper was a map. A map of the battlefield . . . with officers' names and dates . . . created by the National Park Service in the twenty-first century and handed out for free in the Manassas visitors' center.

So that's how he convinced the officers he wasn't just a lunatic. He's been using that map to make predictions all day, and now the officers are starting to believe him.

By now about a hundred men have swarmed to us. I'm glad to see that Big Jim and Elmer are among them and okay. I wonder how their brother is doing.

Cyrus cries out, "See General Bee! We can still join his men." His shout seems to be answered by one from Bee's group. He and his men are about halfway between us and the Yankee line. Wounded and dead Confederates litter the ground behind Bee's charging men, but they've blown big holes in the Union line up ahead of them. They just might do it. Just a little farther . . . a well-placed assault to crush the Union flank and . . .

There's an eerie calm as we wait to hear him yell "Charge!" Suddenly General Bee falls from his horse to the ground. Almost immediately another officer leaps from his horse and is at General Bee's side.

We see General Bee push himself up to his hands and knees, and a cheer erupts from the men around me. I give a shout too, but the cry isn't completely out of my mouth when I see General Bee collapse back to the ground and lie still. The Confederate charge wavers. Men fall all around him.

"We've got to go help them!" cries Cyrus.

"No!" orders the pale-faced officer. "Bee is lost. We have another mission."

He points farther to our left, just north of the Yankee line. It's the hill where Dupree was just looking.

"I have just received intelligence that in a few minutes Union cannons will be wheeled to that spot," the officer says. He glances at Dupree as if for reassurance. Dupree nods. "If they take that hill, they will be able to flank us and bombard our entire line and we will be destroyed. We must take the cannons first."

This plan sounds familiar to me. It seems like I remember reading in one of Dad's history books something about Confederate troops capturing, or trying to capture, some Union artillery. Practically a suicide mission, like General Bee's just now. But I can't recall what they did with the guns once they seized them. One thing I'm sure of—the books never said anything about which of those soldiers ever made it back alive.

Now I'm one of those soldiers. Only my mission is to make their mission fail.

The officer gives the order—"Keep close to the flag!"—and we take off. It's more of a sprint than a march. At the head of our group, a guy is huffing with this Rebel flag in his hands. No gun, just a flag.

The weight of my gun practically topples me over. I'm gasping as we hit the hill. Someone starts shooting at us, but no one gets hit. We hurdle a split-rail fence and disappear into a cornfield.

"Stay together! Stay together!" Cyrus shouts, staying low and cutting through the rows of chest-high corn so fast it's nearly impossible for any of us to stay together. Especially me. This is like having twenty gym classes in a row. And I suck at gym. I'm the last to make it to the far side of the cornfield.

We fall to the ground and peer out through the corn. We're halfway up the short hill where the cannons are supposed to be set up.

"I don't see a durn thing," Cyrus mutters. "Some intelligence."

As if on cue, a team of horses appears over the crest of the hill. The horses haul a cannon behind them. Cyrus gives a low whistle. The officer says, "That's one of them Parrott guns . . . ten pounder . . . big and rifled and real accurate if you know how to use it."

Oh man, a Parrott gun! This thing is like the Tiger Woods of cannons. A lot of Civil War cannons aren't rifled. They're just smooth-bore barrels that fire round balls that don't really spin or rotate or fly real straight. But the Parrott guns have grooved barrels that spin the bullet-shaped ammo, making it fly straighter. These things shoot real far and are real accurate.

And that's what's on the hill ahead of us. Another team of horses crests the hill. Another and another. In all, six teams of horses pulling cannons appear over the top of a low rise. A full battery. Once they're set up, General Jackson's men won't be safe. They'll be easy targets.

Our officer motions us into a line of battle.

"Huh, I guess that intelligence was intelligent after all," Cyrus whispers as he crawls into position. "How did he know?"

I know how he knew. I look around for the officer's "intelligence," but nowhere is the black hat visible. I crane my neck so I can see all the way down the line. Still no Dupree. He's not with us. He didn't come. He's sending us to do his dirty work, whatever it is. I've got a bad feeling that he's come up with a pretty good plan here.

On top of the hill, Yankee soldiers busily untie their horses from the cannons and begin arranging the big guns.

"Everybody loaded?" whispers our officer. "We'll all fire at once and we'll have them before they turn around. Ready, men? On three . . . one . . . two . . . THREE!"

We step out from the corn and open fire. The first ten Yankees to die all get shot in the back.

But not by me. I can't bring myself to do it. I aim my musket just over their heads, just like a reenactor, and pull the trigger. My shoulder practically breaks from the gun's recoil.

Our flag guy leads our charge, but only makes it a few steps when he's hit. I see some Yankees at the top of the hill taking potshots from behind their cannons.

Cyrus grabs the flag from the ground in one hand and with his musket in the other lets out this god-awful scream and charges up the hill. The others beside me follow.

Watching Cyrus run, I don't see how he'll ever get shot in the butt. His backside is never to the enemy. Maybe somehow I've kept it from happening. I don't know if that's good or bad.

All right. Another charge. I'm getting pretty good at this. I take a deep breath and start to take off.

"Yaaagh!" I yell as all of a sudden I'm yanked back into the corn and flat on my back.

"What the . . ." I gasp, trying to catch my breath. The sun's right in my face and all I can see is this looming shadow over me. My gut seizes up. All I can think is *Dupree!* I'm about to really cuss when the shadow drops beside me. My gut takes a different flip. It's Ashby, her freckled face real close to mine.

"I'm sorry," she says, "but I had to tell you something. I caught a little of what he's up to."

My brain feels a little woozy. "Huh?" I say.

"Stonewall!" Ash says. "Please pay attention." She gives me a thump on the head.

"Ow!"

"I'm sorry," she says. "But my father . . . what you guys are doing is part of some sort of stunt he's got up his sleeve."

"Yeah," I say, rubbing my head. "I figured that part out already."

Ash looks through the cornstalks up the hill. I follow and can just see Cyrus, Big Jim, and Elmer wheeling one of the cannons around to aim away from us.

"I was carrying buckets of water to some of the wounded behind the line and that's where I saw him talking . . ."

"Figures he'd be *behind* the line," I sneer.

"Well, it has made it easier for me to keep track of him."

"He didn't see you?" I ask.

She looks down at her dress, sad. "I tried to keep out of his sight . . . but I don't think he's even looking for me. I think he's forgotten about me."

I want to comfort her somehow, but all I can think of is patting her shoulder. Which feels real dorky after I do it, but she does give me a little smile.

"Anyway, I was trying to get as close as I could to my father without him noticing me. He was talking to this one guy who looked like he was in charge of this artillery unit—all these guys around him were cleaning out and loading these big cannons. And my dad was showing him a map!"

"What'd he say?"

"I'm sorry. I couldn't get close enough to hear everything. But I kept hearing them saying the same thing over and over. But it doesn't make any sense."

"What?"

She looks at me like she's not sure of herself. "They kept saying, 'Sure, man.'"

"What?!" I say. "'Sure, man'? These guys don't talk like that. They aren't a bunch of surfer dudes."

Ash shrugs. "I know. But they kept saying it a lot and were real serious and now the officer is marching his men up here right . . ."

She stops.

"What?" I say, but she clamps her hand over my mouth. Not the worse thing in the world.

Now I hear it. Footsteps. From the other end of the corn-field.

Ashby whispers in my ear, "I don't know what he's doing, but you've got to stop it. Please, Stonewall. Hurry!"

Ash crouches low and scurries away down a corn row.

I jump to my feet and run fast up the hill toward Cyrus. He's planted the Confederate flag almost at the top of the hill by an ammunition cart and is now heaving against an artillery piece. I fall in beside him.

"Glad you could make it," he says.

I don't answer, just push. Or at least pretend to.

"Wheel them around!" I hear our officer shout, his white face finally showing some color.

About a hundred yards below us on the other side of the hill is the right flank of the Union line. Now we can do to them what they were planning to do to us. As we turn the cannon around, the history of this moment flashes into my brain. The Confederates did capture the Union artillery, but they didn't have any artillery men as part of the charge. The Confederates never knew how to load and aim the guns, so once they fired the guns already loaded they had to retreat back to their line.

Now I see I'm right. Once we get the cannons turned around, Cyrus and the others are puzzled at what to do next. I've seen it done at the reenactments a gazillion times, but I've always been too busy complaining about the noise to find out how it all works.

One soldier tries yanking one of the horse harness chains still strapped to a cannon. Another dimwit actually sticks his arm down a gun's barrel to feel if it's loaded with a shell. He'd make a good reenactor.

From the ammunition cart behind the cannons, Cyrus picks up a ten-pound iron shell and heaves it through the Parrott's muzzle. But he has no clue where to load the powder and detonate the gun.

"Cease fire!" our officer suddenly commands even though not one of the guns has been shot. "Cease fire!" he shouts again. "That's what they're for." And he points back to the cornfield.

Out of the stalks march twelve Southern soldiers, muskets on their right shoulders, led by another officer. Only when they reach us, stack their muskets, and deploy two men to each of the six cannons do I recognize the new officer's bushy blond sideburns and a fat belly. He was the other one that Dupree approached . . . the one who Ashby must have seen with her father.

Now I see. Dupree knows all too well this part of the battle. So he's made sure this time the Confederates have people who can work the Parrott guns.

As I watch the new troops methodically load and prime the artillery, I get the feeling I'm still missing something. Why would Dupree do this? He and I already know that the South wins this battle. Whether it happens with or without the Parrott guns shouldn't really matter. Should it?

Down below the hill, General Jackson's men have begun an assault of their own. They have pushed the Yankee line back to Mrs. Henry's house, but are now pinned down themselves. A few volleys from our artillery could clear the way for General Jackson to crush the Union line once and for all.

I look back to our guns and brace for their blasts. A few seconds pass. But nothing happens. I look to the artillery officer, expecting him to order his men to fire. But he's not even facing them. He's holding to his eye a long old-fashioned brass telescope—at least, it's old-fashioned looking to me.

"Do you see him?" our pale-faced officer asks.

The fat one shakes his head.

"But he said he'd be right there by the house."

"I know what he said!" the fat one snaps. "But maybe he doesn't know everything. I mean, who can say for sure where someone would be at any particular time on a particular battlefield? Especially with Sherman."

Cyrus glances at me. "Who the heck is Sherman?"

Sherman? I'm too surprised to answer Cyrus. Not *sure, man. Sherman!* Ash had been thrown off by the officer's thick Southern drawl.

I'd forgotten that Sherman was here . . . no, *is* here, at Manassas. Of all the Yankees, William T. Sherman is the one most hated in the South. Later in the war, he will burn and destroy much of the South—houses, schools, crops, cattle, most of Atlanta, anything on his "March to the Sea" as it's eventually called—as part of a plan to crush the spirit of the Confederates back home. Even I don't like him. He is a terrible man with a terrible job ahead of him. But I also know it's a job that needs to be done for the North to win the war.

Dupree must know he's down there somewhere. So he's

gotten these two Rebel yahoos to capture the guns that can do the job: Scout Sherman out and kill him. And if Sherman goes, so does one crucial piece of the Union puzzle that will one day win the war. Who knows? Maybe like a domino game, his fall leads to other Yankee losses.

"Got him!" says the artillery officer, peering through his telescope. He's standing next to the artillerymen's musket stack, and the other officer steps quickly to his side.

"Are you sure?" he asks.

"Durn sure I'm sure," the artillery officer replies. "He was in my class at the Point." He hands off the scope. "Look for yourself."

While his companion looks, the artillery officer barks orders to his men—coordinates, range, altitude. Any moment they'll have a lock on Sherman, or as close to a lock as Civil War cannon can have.

The science fiction scenarios tumble through my mind. I'm pretty sure I haven't done anything today to change the outcome of the battle, the war. But what am I supposed to do when someone else wants just that—a different ending? Let it happen?

Seriously, what *am* I supposed to do, shoot the officer? How can I shoot a real live person? But what if that person is unknowingly going to change the world, let the South win and all the crap that comes with that? No, I still can't shoot him. But what? Step in front of their guns? They'd either yank me away or just blow me up. I can't overpower the whole battery by myself.

Sweat drips down my face. I look behind me. The stack of muskets! Maybe I can grab a couple of muskets and sneak off somewhere and fire them and create some kind of diversion that'll bring the others running and stop them from doing what they want to do. It's not much, but . . .

Wait a second. Just beyond the stack of muskets, I see what I need.

Quietly, I take a step backward. Another and another. The eyes of all the other Confederates around me are down below, looking in the direction of the big guns. Three more steps and I'm at the ammunition cart. I grab the staff of the Confederate flag and pull it out of the ground. I carefully climb onto the cart. Standing about four feet above the heads of Cyrus and all the others, I'm now the tallest point on this hill. Still none of the Confederates see me—I hope to God some of the Yankees do. I take a deep breath, thrust the flag high up in the air and start to wave it.

The two officers standing to the left of the six guns are gazing at the enemy below. "Ready, men!" I hear the artillery officer yell. The last gun grinds into place. "Aim!" I see Big Jim and Elmer put their hands to their ears. I wave my flag as hard as I can. The artillery officer raises his hand.

BOOM!

The earth shakes and I fall to the ground. Fire and smoke envelop us. Chunks of dirt and rock land on my back. I look up to the officers. Where they were standing is now a gaping hole from an artillery shell. The nearest gun to them is a twisted mass of metal. The rest of our men are alive but on the ground. They look like drunks as they stagger back on their feet.

Only Cyrus seems collected. Through the smoky haze, I see him scrambling from soldier to soldier. He pulls them to their feet and hands them their guns again. He's pointing down the hill and yelling at the men to get into a battle line.

The smoke lifts. I look to where Cyrus gestures. A determined horde of Yankees is charging up a lane right at us. An officer urging them on, they're coming to get their cannons back. Whether they saw my flag or had already seen us, or were simply doing what my history books say they actually did, I don't know. A small part of me hopes it was my flag. But a bigger part—the part that remembers the Yankee shell hitting our two officers—hopes I had nothing to do with it.

The Yankees get closer and closer. Our artillery guys still look dazed. They're also unarmed. The shell that killed the officers also obliterated their muskets. They take one look at the advancing enemy, one look at each other, and bolt toward the cornfield, disappearing into the stalks.

"I guess it's up to us," Cyrus says. "I was hoping for a chance to shoot off one of these. True, I'm not sure exactly how to go about it."

Cyrus, Big Jim, and Elmer stand over one of the cannons. For a second they look like some of my neighbors staring into the engine of a pickup truck. Cyrus holds a smoldering stick.

"Maybe if you light it here," I hear Elmer say.

Cyrus touches the stick to where Elmer points. Nothing happens.

I try to estimate the number of men coming at us. Two

hundred maybe? Five hundred? A glance at our line and it's obviously more than us.

"Uh, Cyrus, the Yankees are getting closer," I say. "Lots of 'em."

Cyrus glances at me. His face is almost black from gunpowder, and he's bleeding from a scrape on his scalp. But his eyes are steady as they look at me. He smiles.

"Good," he says, "the closer the better. I'm not sure exactly how to aim this thing either."

Suddenly Elmer screams and falls to the ground. He clutches his arm. Blood pumps from a bullet hole, his white sleeve turns scarlet.

"I'm not turning yellow, Cyrus," I say again, "but they've got us outnumbered. Let's leave all this and get Elmer some help."

"Are you kidding? At this range we can't miss!"

"But we don't even know how to fire—"

BOOM! Cyrus's gun recoils. Smoke gushes from the barrel. Somehow he's figured it out. Or maybe he accidentally touched the fuse. He grins. But the shot zooms right over the Yankees' heads. Now they are within easy musket range and they open fire on us. We dive for cover. No chance we can even get off another shot.

"Come on," I plead. "They're going to get these guns one way or another. If we make it back to our line we can keep fighting!"

This idea appeals to the others, especially since Elmer is starting to turn pale from loss of blood. Cyrus reluctantly agrees. We take off back the way we came. At least this time we're going downhill. Elmer can barely run, so Big Jim half carries him.

We plunge through the cornfield and make it back to our old line, where we collapse into a small crater created by an exploded shell. Big Jim screams for an orderly to take care of Elmer, but there doesn't seem to be one around.

I turn to look for Cyrus. He's gone. I look back the way we came.

Oh, no.

He has stopped halfway down the slope and is standing straight up in the middle of the cornfield, his red head and shoulders sticking out like a balloon over the crop. Good grief! He's loading his gun! Bullets whiz by all around him, cutting ears of corn from their stalks.

"What are you doing?" I scream, but he can't hear me.

I watch in horror as he takes aim and fires. The advancing Yankees have now reached the cannons we just abandoned and are wheeling them back around at us. What can Cyrus possibly do all by himself? He must be crazy!

I see him start loading his gun again. I have no choice. I run back into the open to get him. A bullet buzzes by my ear as I dive into the corn.

"What are you doing?" I holler when I get to him.

"What does it look like I'm doing?" he says, taking aim again. I follow the line of his gun right up to the ammunition cart. He squeezes the trigger.

A huge blast erupts from the artillery. At first it seems like one of the cannons has opened fire on us. But when the smoke clears, I see I'm wrong. Cyrus must have hit one of the powder kegs, and now a fire rages from the ammunition cart. Two dead Yankees slump over one gun and others run away.

I look wide-eyed at Cyrus.

"Hated to leave all that powder for them Yanks," he says. "You have to agree—that was a durn good shot."

CHAPTER TEN

WE DIVE back into the crater with Big Jim and Elmer and lie still a moment trying to catch our breath. Just as we stop gasping, more bugles ring out over the battlefield. I peek over the crater's edge. A brigade of Yankees has just joined the Union line by the Henry House.

I turn to warn the others, but Cyrus is crouched over Elmer. Elmer is lying on the ground, his face white and eyes rolling into the back of his head. I thought he was just grazed in the arm, but now I see that the shot practically amputated him at the elbow. His sleeve and the right half of his white shirt are drenched in blood. I wonder if it really matters if he makes it to the doctor. From what I know about battlefield medicine, he doesn't stand much of a chance.

All of a sudden, Cyrus jumps up.

"Get down!" I yell. Cyrus has his back to the enemy and is scanning the rear of our line. Without warning he starts jumping up and down and waving, as if he's trying to be the target of the entire Union army.

"Cyrus!" I cry as I hear bullets buzzing overhead. Maybe this is it. Maybe this is where he gets the butt shot. But just as quickly, he's back on the ground beside me.

"Big Jim, I can see a nurse just back of the line a bit. You've got to get Elmer out of here," says Cyrus as he finishes tying off a handkerchief around Elmer's arm in a vain effort to stop the bleeding. "He's not up for this."

Big Jim doesn't move, just lies stretched out next to Elmer.

"Go on, Big Jim," Cyrus says again.

Big Jim looks up at Cyrus. Gunpowder has turned his face just about as black as his hair and wiry beard, but now I see tears trickling down his cheeks, leaving clean streaks where they run.

"You don't think . . . that John Mark could have done this?" he says, more of a statement than a question.

Cyrus tries to smile. "He ain't that good of a shot, Big Jim. Now go."

Big Jim slings Elmer's good arm around his neck and begins to stand. He doesn't make it far. Big Jim's leg buckles and both men crumple to the ground.

"Big Jim, what the . . ."

And now we see it. Blood seeping up Big Jim's shirt from his waist. Cyrus pulls up Big Jim's shirt to see where a bullet has struck his hip.

"I'll be okay," Big Jim gasps. "Just a scratch."

Cyrus whips out the flask from his back pocket and gives it to Big Jim. Big Jim raises it like he's toasting Cyrus and takes a long swig.

"Whoa!" Big Jim gasps. "Some strong stuff, Cyrus."

"Can you walk?" Cyrus asks.

Big Jim nods. "I can walk. I just can't carry."

Cyrus slips under Elmer's other arm. "Stonewall, take Big Jim's place."

Big Jim gently lifts his brother's arm and places it on my shoulder. My legs buckle, but I hold on.

"C'mon," Cyrus says, and we start moving toward the rear.

Confederate soldiers pass us heading to the firing line.

"We'll be back with you in a minute, boys!" Cyrus tells them.

Yeah, we certainly wouldn't want to get too far away from all these lovely bullets.

Maybe it's a lull in the battle, but it gets quieter with every step we take toward the rear. We come to another hole in the ground that's been gouged out by an explosion and carefully lay out Elmer. Big Jim collapses beside him. I hit the ground too, but Cyrus stands back up and waves his arms to something or someone farther back.

"I got 'em," he says. "They're coming."

Before I can ask who, two black kids scurry up with a stretcher between them. I hardly notice them because right on their heels is a nurse.

Ashby.

She kneels beside Elmer and starts wrapping his wound. Cyrus backs away to let her work, but not me.

She leans close to me and whispers, "Good job. Dad was furious when the Yankees got the guns back."

I don't say anything. My stomach is all twisted and my eyes keep seeing the hole where the two officers stood. Did I do that?

She glances at me. "You okay?"

I try to nod, to look soldierly, whatever that means. Instead I feel tears on my face. "Yeah, I'm fine. But those two officers died back there."

Ash looks away and ties a knot on Elmer's bandage. "I'm sorry, Stonewall."

I wipe my face with the back of my sleeve so it looks like I'm just wiping away sweat. "Let's just say it wasn't the greatest idea I've ever had."

"But it worked, didn't it? My father will do whatever it takes, so we have to do whatever it takes too."

Suddenly Big Jim lets out a yell. We look, and the two stretcher bearers are trying to pick him up.

"Not me," Big Jim snaps at them. "Him."

The boys look at Elmer. "He's dead," one boy says.

"Not yet," says Big Jim. "Get him, *nigger.*"

Did he just say *the* word—the N-word? Shocked, I look up at Big Jim. But I don't think he even realizes he's said something awful. Neither does Cyrus and neither do the two boys . . . I guess they've heard it all their lives.

But Ash looks at me and I can tell we're both feeling the same thing.

The boys reposition the stretcher beside Elmer, who now lies still. Only the jerky rise and fall of his chest proves he's alive.

I move out of the way so the boy closest to me can grab

Elmer's feet. I look into the boy's straining face and am surprised to recognize him.

"Jacob," I say.

The boy glances at me.

"Jacob, how did you—"

"Move, boy!" Big Jim shouts.

"Look, Cyrus," I say. "It's Jacob."

I can't explain to Cyrus or anyone why I'm excited to see Jacob. Maybe it's because he seems about my age. Maybe because he, like me, has been living this boring life, minding his own business, doing what he's told until suddenly waking up this morning to find himself in the middle of a huge battle.

But Cyrus clearly doesn't seem interested. "Who?" he asks. "Who cares? Move it!"

Jacob and the other boy lift the heavy stretcher.

"Thank you, Jacob," I whisper. "I'm glad you're here."

He looks at me and smiles. But it's that fake smile again, the same he gave in Mrs. Henry's house. It's the kind I gave my parents when I got my own set of camping utensils for Christmas instead of *Grand Theft Auto*. I watch him and the other boy lift up Elmer and walk off into the cedar trees behind us, and wonder if Jacob even knows how to really smile.

I feel a pat on my shoulder. "I've got to go, Stonewall," Ash whispers in my ear. "Watch out for my father. And I'll do the same."

In a louder voice, she says, "You boys take care of each other."

Cyrus tips his hat. "You take care too, ma'am."

Ash smiles at him and runs off after Jacob.

"Whew," says Cyrus, grinning wildly, "I've read about girls that beautiful, but I never seen one before. Shall I compare her to a summer's day?"

"No thanks," says Big Jim. "I think you need to turn around here and look at what's coming at you, not what's leaving."

We turn around and I realize that we are in a world of hurt. A wave of Yankees is charging and I know that many more are coming. I also know that many Confederates will die trying to hold them off. Me and Cyrus and Big Jim might very well be among them. Before either side gives up, there is going to be a lot of bloodshed—maybe ours.

I wish I could stop all this. To tell General McDowell and all the other Yankees not to bother. That their assault will cost a lot of lives on both sides, but not succeed. I hate being a part of this.

Why would anyone want to reenact something this stupid?

A fresh attack has started. Another wave of McDowell's men. We counter it and push them back. They counter us and the whole thing starts over again. As the afternoon wears on and the sun gets lower in the sky, the only thing that really changes is the number of wounded and dead.

It's a miracle Cyrus isn't killed. He never misses a chance to expose himself to enemy fire. But he is a crack shot if his gun is in range. He's hit at least a dozen Yankees so far today. I on the other hand just keep going through the motions. Loading my gun, shooting just a little too high. Trying to dodge the bullets and balls.

Finally a cry goes up.

"Look back there!" hollers Big Jim. He's echoed by probably a hundred other soldiers.

We look south. At least a thousand Confederates are marching up the dirt road to join our line. They have traveled by train a hundred miles from the Shenandoah Valley and are ready to fight. I have been waiting for this moment . . . and dreading it.

I know these new Confederates will create a tidal wave of soldiers that will wash the Yankees halfway back to Washington. I know Cyrus will want to be near the front of our attack. I think about trying to explain to him about the future again, but I figure that's a waste of time. I wish I could stop him from getting killed. But maybe it has to happen. I just don't know and there's never any time to think.

The pounding of horses' hoofs shakes the ground beneath our feet. I turn around just in time to see General Jackson rein in his horse a few feet from my face.

"Give me a battle line!" he orders. At once, both wounded and well soldiers jolt to their feet and into formation. Even Big Jim, who seems to forget he's been shot in the hip, jumps when he sees General Jackson.

General Jackson draws his sword and points it at Mrs. Henry's house. Still surrounding it are Union soldiers who resembled a wild sea earlier in the day but after several hours of battle now look like a bunch of puddles.

General Jackson stands up in his stirrups. A bullet shoots

his hat from his head but he doesn't even flinch. "This is the moment!" he thunders. "Our moment! And when you charge, yell like Furies!"

Suddenly the world stops—the guns, the cannon fire, the cries of wounded men. Everything grows quiet as all eyes focus on him. I catch my breath, waiting for the order, even wishing for it so I can start to breathe again.

And it comes.

"Charge!"

The reenactors always talk of the Rebel yell, that whooping holler of noise that Confederate soldiers supposedly made as they rushed into a fight. The noise, according to the books, made the Yankees tremble with fear. I could never understand why, judging from the silly "yeehaws" that croaked from my father and his friends at their reenactments.

But this—

The only word to describe the shrieking that drives our charge is unholy. The demonic screams seem to pick us up and carry us the first hundred yards toward the Henry House. When I feel my feet again I am within range of the Yankees' muskets. It should be easy for them to blast holes in our line.

But nothing comes. Their faces that once seemed so determined are now terrified. They drop their guns, abandon their artillery, and flee from the house and down Henry Hill. Moments later we reach their big guns, and this time we have a leader who knows what to do.

Before the war, General Jackson was an artillery instructor. Several units of his men step forward, turn the guns around, and aim them down the hill at the panicked, fleeing soldiers.

"Fire at will," General Jackson calls. And the cries that led our charge are now answered by the booming of our new guns. The result of each is the same. Fright. Fear. A wild retreat. And victory for the South.

CHAPTER ELEVEN

THE UNION retreat is this totally screwed-up scramble across any ford or bridge to get over Bull Run and back on the road to Washington. There is no rearguard to protect the retreating Yankees from the Confederate attack. They are in chaos.

The only thing that's saving them is the fact that the Rebels' pursuit is just as nuts. Confederates stop at every dead Yankee to pick his pockets. They swipe watches, coins, bullets, and powder boxes. We pass one guy unlacing some soldier's shoes. Even luckier Rebels are dumping their old-fashioned muskets in exchange for the Enfield rifles, but only after prying loose the clutching fingers of the dead Yankees who brought them into battle.

"Scavengers," Cyrus mutters, though I do catch him looking forlornly at his old musket.

He and I are among the few who have stayed in a ragged line of battle. Big Jim is with us too, but he seems to limp more with every step as we march steadily along behind the fleeing Yanks. They are tramping along the Warrenton Turnpike, and though they're only a few hundred yards ahead of us, we are pretty safe. They aren't shooting at us and we aren't really shooting at them. It's like they're glad just to be rid of the battlefield and we're glad just to do the ridding.

"Feel like I'm back home herding cattle," says Cyrus. "Over yonder across Bull Run is the corral and that bridge there is the gate. Get them across there and they'll head for home."

The Henry House smolders in the distance behind us. Its white, two-story wood frame is pocked with cannon and bullet holes like the surface of the moon. Beside it, a silhouette in the setting sun, I can see a man with a shovel digging a hole in the yard. A grave for Mrs. Henry, I suppose. I hope her death was peaceful.

"Pipe tobacco and coffee! Get 'em while they're hot!"

The voice comes from our right. I look and see a short, plump man with a full red beard. He wears a black suit with a bow tie and is pushing a cart with a jangling cow bell down a lane and right into our path. Soldiers limp to the man and plunk coins into his hand.

"My name is Wilmer McLean and I'm here to ease your pain."

Big Jim stays back, resting on his musket and watching the horizon. Cyrus picks up a packet of tobacco and sniffs it. For the first time today I notice that he has a corncob pipe bulging out of his back pocket, the one not holding the flask.

"McLean," I murmur. "Seems like I should know that name."

McLean's eyes pop wide in fake surprise and he takes a hop backward. "My reputation doth precede me. Perhaps you have patronized my store in town. Or have reposed in my inn?"

I shake my head.

"Well," he continues, "you are standing near McLean soil." He points behind him. "Just over that hill is my barn, which your army—er, my country—has chosen for its temporary medical residence. Rent-free, I should add. I am, after all, a patriot."

Now it clicks. Wilmer McLean, owner of part of the Manassas battlefield where the war's first fight took place . . . is taking place.

"Yes sir," McLean continues. "For years and years my domain exists in bucolic tranquility and then one day I wake up and find forty thousand men tromping by my house. Total chaos."

Yeah, right. You really seem to be suffering from all this chaos. How much money have you made today? You're even worse than those sutlers who rip off tourists at the reenactments.

"So may I interest you gentlemen in my wares?" he asks while plucking the packet of tobacco from Cyrus's hand.

Cyrus takes a long look at the tobacco. "Ain't got any money on me," he says.

I dig around in my pockets. No coins. Of course, even if I did have money, it wouldn't be the kind that McLean would recognize.

McLean shakes his head and clucks his tongue. "Then I'm afraid, sir, that you don't have any tobacco on you either . . . unless . . ." McLean eyes the knives on Cyrus's belt, ". . . you'd be willing to part with your blades."

Cyrus puts a protective hand over each hilt. "No sale."

McLean shrugs. "So be it," he says, and with that, McLean pushes his cart away.

Cyrus is pretty grumpy as we keep marching.

"Been risking my life all day for that bastard and his barn," I hear him grumbling, "and he can't spare a pipeful of tobacco. Some patriot."

I almost tell him that McLean's the kind of guy who one day will be a Civil War reenactor, but he wouldn't understand. We walk a few minutes and an idea pops into my head. I stop and tell Cyrus, "You go on. I'll catch up in a minute."

I'm about to turn back, but Cyrus stops too. His eyes narrow.

"I promise," I tell him. "I told you I'm not running now."

Cyrus studies me another second, cracks a smile, and starts marching again.

I jog back to McLean's cart.

"Pipe tobacco and coffee!" he cries out. "Wounded and maimed get ten percent off!"

I step to the front of the line. "Five packets of your finest tobacco," I say.

Now McLean's eyes pop wide for real. "Five packets!" he declares. "Why, even the goodly, nay, saintly General Bee only purchased three this morning before he met his untimely demise."

He licks his lips. "And how might you pay for this?"

"A trade?" I say.

McLean squints. "And what could you possibly have that I might want?

I reach into my satchel. "An e-lectric music box," I say, and I hold out my Game Boy. I flip it on and it flashes and beeps out the theme of *Orc Slayer 2059*.

McLean's eyes bug out like golf balls. He reaches out and carefully takes it from my hands. He brings it closer to his eyes, to his ears. He even sniffs it.

"Yes, boy," he whispers. "Five packets seem just about right."

As I walk away, I wonder for a moment if I've made a mistake. A twenty-first-century Game Boy in the wrong nineteenth-century hands? But the batteries *are* almost dead. I doubt McLean will be changing any history with it.

I march back down the lane to find Cyrus and Big Jim. It doesn't take long. I spot them standing beside another house, much smaller than Mrs. Henry's, really just one big room with a small front porch. I've seen the house before, but I know it wasn't there the last time my parents dragged me to Manassas. On that part of the battlefield, only the Henry House still stands.

I reach Cyrus's side, but he and Big Jim don't seem to realize I'm here. I follow their gaze to a dead Yankee slumped against the front porch. He's young, about Cyrus's age, with long blond curls and a smooth white face.

Lying faceup at his feet is a comrade of his, shot in the stomach and dead too. He has black curly hair and a mustache. Something about his pale face looks familiar. But there's something in all the dead soldiers I've seen today that looks familiar. Maybe it's how surprised they all look—their eyes opened wide or eyebrows wrinkled—like they didn't really expect today to be this bad.

125

"Cyrus," I say, and reach into my satchel for the tobacco. "I got you some—"

Before I can finish, Big Jim falls to his knees. He grabs the black-haired Yankee's shirt and buries his face into his chest. He starts crying loud, painful sobs that shake him and the Yankee's body.

And it hits me why the Yankee looks familiar. He looks like Big Jim and Elmer. This must be John Mark, their older brother, who didn't believe in the secession and went to fight with the North.

I've seen a lot of fear and death today. But seeing Big Jim clutching his brother brings tears to my eyes. I take a step toward him to pat his shoulder when all of a sudden he jumps up and runs to the other dead Yankee leaning against the house and starts screaming and punching the corpse in the ribs.

In an instant, Cyrus is behind him. He seizes Big Jim's collar and yanks him away.

"Leave me be!" Big Jim cries.

But Cyrus doesn't leave him be. He spins Big Jim around, throws his arms around his shoulders, and hugs him tightly. Big Jim fights against Cyrus, hits him a few times hard in the back. But Cyrus doesn't let go. He just squeezes harder until Big Jim finally sinks onto Cyrus's shoulder and begins weeping again.

I step over to the dead Yankee's battered corpse. I guess Big Jim blames this kid and all the other Union soldiers here for going to war over the secession and causing John Mark to make a choice. Fight for his brothers or fight for his country. I'm glad I'll never have to make a choice like that.

Just as I'm about to turn away, I notice a scrap of paper clutched in the Yankee's hand. I kneel down and start peeling his rigid fingers from the paper. It's an envelope.

When I work it free, I see scrawled on the envelope the name Sarah. It's not sealed, so I open it carefully and take out the page. It's dated July 14, 1861. One week ago today.

My dear Sarah, We shall move in a few days, perhaps tomorrow. Lest I should not be able to write you again, I feel impelled to write a few lines that may fall under your eye when I shall be no more.

Now, this reads like science fiction. I mean, the guy writes like he knows he's going to die. Like he's already dead. As I keep reading, though, the letter turns from strange to simply sad. First, the guy tells his wife he's ready to die for his government, for his country. That he feels a debt to all those men who have died before him to make the country great.

But then he says he knows his death will mean sorrow for his wife. That he's glad to have spent so much time with her, but that he will miss being with her and watching his sons grow up.

By the time I read his last sentence, I am crying.

My dear Sarah, never forget how much I love you, and when my last breath escapes me on the battlefield, it will whisper your name.
Sullivan

From the look of his wounds, he never got the chance to whisper her name. You never see this part in the reenactments, with all their dramatic cries of anguish and overacted death scenes. This is a real man who gave up everything for his ideals, for his country. But why did this man's wife, Sarah, have to suffer for this to come true? Surely there was a better way to make America great than for thousands of men to kill each other in Mrs. Henry's front yard.

I have to keep my back turned to Cyrus and Big Jim so they can't see the tears trickling down my cheeks. Can't let them catch me crying over a Yankee I don't know. I fold the letter, put it back in the envelope, and slip it into the soldier's pocket. Maybe a friend will come back and find him and know how to find Sarah. She will want to read it.

As I kneel beside Sullivan, a shadow falls over us. I look up to find Edward, the black man who took care of Mrs. Henry, standing over me. Sweat drenches his bald, shining head and he is wiping mud and dirt off his hands with a handkerchief.

"What are you doing here?" I ask.

"My house," he replies.

And I know where I've seen this house before. This is the Robinson House. I've seen it in pictures in history books, but only its foundation survives to the time my family visited the field. And the man staring into his muddy black hands must be Mr. Robinson, a freed slave.

"You're Mr. Robinson," I say.

This gets him looking up. "How you know that?"

Before I know what I'm saying, I hear the words come from my mouth. "Because I'm not one of them."

I'm not sure what I mean, and I don't know if Mr. Robinson does either. But he nods as if he understands and keeps wiping his hands.

I ask, "How is Mrs. Henry?"

He shrugs. "Soon to be in the ground. I just dug the hole."

I don't know if I should or not, but I reply, "I'm sorry."

He nods again.

"Does she have any family?" I ask.

"Just her son," he answers, "ever since our father died."

This sounds strange. "Our?" I ask.

"Me and Missus Henry's," he says.

Now I am totally confused. "But that means she's your sister," I say. "How, if you're, well . . . and she's, like . . ."

He spits into his hands and keeps wiping. "My momma was Mr. Henry's housekeeper and when I was born I was his slave as well as his son. But his daughter, Judith, she never treated me like a slave. She treated me like a brother. Now she's gone too."

"And that's why you were freed when your father died," I say.

He just shrugs again. "Suppose so, but the problem is Jacob. Mrs. Henry owned him and treated him all right. I don't know what'll happen to him now."

He picks up his shovel and walks back toward the remains of Mrs. Henry's house.

I want to call out to him not to worry. That Jacob—and all the other slaves—will be free in just a few years when the war is over. But he would just think I was crazy.

"Thank you, ma'am, thank you very much," I hear Big Jim saying.

I turn to see Ash again. She's bent over John Mark's body, wiping the blood from his face and closing his eyes. I imagine she's done that many times today. It's the first time I really stop to think that she's been through stuff that may be even worse than what I've had to do.

She pats Big Jim on the arm and stands up. I walk over to meet her. Cyrus gives me a look and turns back to Big Jim.

"How are you?" she asks with this real intense look on her face.

"Okay," I whisper. "Tired, really. Real tired. You?"

"Yeah," she says. "The same." She looks around, down at Sullivan, at John Mark and Big Jim. "War sucks."

I want to take her hand, but I can't bring myself to do it. "At least we made it," I tell her. "At least we won."

She looks up at me again. "I'm not so sure."

"What do you mean?"

She turns and points down the lane. At first I can't see what she's talking about. Confederate soldiers are still walking down the turnpike in the direction of the retreating Yankees.

"I don't . . ." I start, and suddenly see it. The black hat . . . the voice . . .

Crap. Dupree.

"Well . . ." I say. "The battle's over. The South won, just like it should. Which means we won. So . . . uh . . . what else can he do?"

But even as I say it, I don't quite buy it. And by the look on her face, neither does Ash.

We watch as Dupree moves from soldier to soldier. He's walking straight and talking loud and doesn't sound at all like a guy who's been beaten. Just when it seems like we've survived this mess and can go home, he wants to keep fighting. I'm tempted to just let him go. I watch as he kneels down next to a wounded Confederate and see the pistol strapped to his ankle. The Weapon. The Tempest. I think about what I wanted to tell Mr. Robinson. About the war being over and Jacob being free.

I just can't imagine it. I just can't imagine Jacob growing up as a slave. Heck, I haven't even really accepted the fact that he's a slave right now. It's too crazy to think about.

"If my father's this excited . . ." Ash says.

I finish her thought. "We're still in trouble."

"So," Ash says.

"So," I say. "Once more into the brink."

"I'll see what I can do to help," she says. "Just remember, don't blow that bugle without me! You could be my ride home." And she runs off to tend to a soldier with a big gash in his leg.

I walk back to Cyrus.

"Looks like something's up," I say, pointing at the soldiers. "You're not going to miss out, are you?"

"Heck, no," says Cyrus, but his grin isn't quite as wide and crazy as usual. He stands and grabs his gun. But Big Jim stays kneeling beside his brother. Cyrus pats Big Jim's shoulder.

"Be back soon, my friend," Cyrus says. And for the first time today, Cyrus looks like he may actually cry.

But his eyes dry up before we're ten steps down the road. We mix in with the soldiers clustered around Dupree.

"Battle's not over yet, boys. There's a couple of Yankee big shots down there. Come and help me round 'em up."

I do the last thing in the world I want to do and pull my hat down and join them.

The Battle of Bull Run may be over, but Dupree's still fighting. And so is his daughter—so I guess I am too.

CHAPTER TWELVE

DUPREE DOES a pretty good imitation of an officer. Somehow the soldiers around me are calling him "colonel," and the act is good enough to fool a lot of the other soldiers we pass. We had fallen behind the first battle line, but Dupree prods many of the stragglers and scavengers into following him.

We start marching east toward Bull Run. In the distance we can see that the Yankees are crossing a small stone bridge—*the* Stone Bridge, as it will one day be known.

Union troops still hold the bridge and Union artillery booms from the stream's far bank, keeping the Confederates from crossing over and harassing the Yankees as they flee back to Washington. But even from where we stand half a mile away, we can see that the Confederates aren't the only people slowing the Union retreat.

In the history books I've read, all the attention is on the soldiers and the fighting. Occasionally the books mention other stuff like the supply trains—hundreds of wagons, pulled by teams of horses and stretching for miles, which carried the soldiers' food, ammunition, tents, medical supplies, and artillery. But I never knew much about them.

Until now. Now that I'm seeing a supply train I realize what a slow-moving nightmare it is. Particularly if the road isn't clear. And right now, it's not.

In the way are a bunch of the Northern officials—senators, congressmen, businessmen, and their wives. This morning they took carriage rides from Washington to Manassas to see their army destroy the Rebels, and with them, the Confederacy. They didn't expect that the Rebels would do the destroying. Now they are all trying to escape back to their homes along with the soldiers. And the road is one big traffic jam.

"There we go, boys, easy pickings!" shouts Dupree, and he picks up the pace.

We keep marching, and by the time we get to the main pack of Confederate troops, the Union fire has slacked off. The traffic jam has straightened out a bit and the Union artillery is being pulled away. The Confederates don't start chasing them again, though.

I know they should, because this is one of the South's best chances of crushing the Union army and winning the war.

Dupree knows this too.

"Keep on their heels, men!" he cries. "Let's teach them to stay out of Our Land!"

More and more soldiers are joining Dupree now.

By the time we start to cross the bridge, there's like a thousand of us. Cyrus and I are somewhere in the middle of the pack and we have to walk three to a row to squeeze across the narrow bridge.

On the other side is a field of corn, probably as tall as me, with the road running through it. The retreating Yankees are still within our sight, most of the Confederate officers are giving orders to capture wounded Yankees who can't keep up with the retreat.

But that's not what Dupree has in mind.

"Who gives a flick about these men?" he says as a line of exhausted, limping Yankees marches by under guard. "We're after bigger game . . . And there it is! C'mon, men!"

He starts us running toward a small group of soldiers. They've captured a small, balding man with a white goatee. He looks like a butler, dressed in a tuxedo with long black coattails.

"Help! Help!" he cries out. "I am a United States congressman!"

A big, red-faced major has a gun leveled at his chest. "And you're still a prisoner of war," he declares.

"Then why are you firing at me?" whimpers the congressman. "A poor old unarmed man? A civilian?"

"That was a mistake," the major answers. "Now come forward and you will be shown honor."

"Honor?" bellows Dupree as he runs up. The major turns around. "This man has no honor and we owe him none! He'll keep fighting until he's in his grave. So take your best shot, soldier."

He slaps Cyrus on the back. Cyrus raises his gun, but hesitates.

"Just shoot him, sir?" says Cyrus.

"Yes, soldier," barks Dupree. His imitation of a real, bloodthirsty colonel is a little too good. Even so, Cyrus still doesn't pull the trigger.

"Don't do it, Cyrus," I whisper. "It's wrong. For a whole lot of reasons."

"What's that, soldier?" snarls Dupree.

I'm terrified that Dupree will recognize me, but I can't back down now.

"Uh, there are rules about prisoners, aren't there?" I say, "I mean, you can't just kill them."

"He's right, sir," says the major, "I can't allow this prisoner to be shot. There are rules to war."

Dupree nods again to the major. "Rules, you say?" His voice is soft. It's the grandfatherly voice. He's campaigning now. This is when he's most dangerous.

"Perhaps today there are rules. But what about tomorrow? Next month? Next year? What about at Antietam when our blood will turn red the road beneath our feet? What about two years from now at Gettysburg when they will butcher thousands of Pickett's men on the field? Or the next year at Petersburg when they blow up a mine they've dug under us?"

Dupree turns around, his arms wide as if to take in all of us who are listening. "We have a chance to end this war now!" he says, his voice now sounding like the preacher. "We kill this man, this"—he glances at the congressman and snarls— "this politician, and the invaders will know we are serious. Deadly serious. The Yankee Congress will lose its will and they will give us what we seek. Freedom!"

Dupree finishes and everyone is silent. I can't tell whether they're in awe of him or just trying to figure out what the heck he's talking about. No one moves as Dupree takes Cyrus's musket. He aims it at the congressman, who has taken shelter behind the major.

"Step aside, major," Dupree says. "And let's see if we can end this war today."

Dupree's preacher voice has done some kind of Jedi mind trick on the major. He steps aside like he's in a trance. The congressman is an easy target. Nobody else is going to help him, obviously, but I'll be durned if I know what to do.

Maybe I can try some kind of professional wrestling move on Dupree. Or club him in the head with my musket. Yesterday I couldn't imagine doing something like that. But . . .

A clattering of hooves rings out from the stone bridge behind us. The major shakes his head as if to wake up.

"What is going on here?" the horseman calls.

Everyone turns, including Dupree. Reining to a stop is a man with a hawk face, bright eyes, and red, brushed-back hair. In place of a uniform, he wears a long gray coat and polished leather riding boots. He looks familiar. But I don't recognize him until Dupree kneels and whispers, "Your Excellency. This is truly an honor."

Jefferson Davis, president of the Confederate States of America, leaps from his horse and grabs the awestruck Dupree by the shoulder and stands him up.

"Please, please, please," President Davis says. "This isn't England and I am no king. A simple 'Mister President' will do just fine."

Turning to the major, President Davis asks, "Now what is amiss here, major?"

"I had this here civilian prisoner in my custody, sir. He'd surrendered." With a nod toward Dupree, the major adds, "But he makes a pretty good case for shooting him."

President Davis looks down to where the congressman is struggling to get back to his feet.

"Alfred?" President Davis says. "Alfred Ely, is that you?"

The congressman stands up and wipes the dust from his white pants. "Aye, Jeff. It's me."

President Davis sticks out his hand and the congressman shakes it. I realize that of course the two men know each other. Before the war, Jefferson Davis was a United States senator from Mississippi, I think. He and Alfred Ely both served in the Capitol in Washington, D.C. They probably attended the same parties and worked on the same laws. Now they are enemies.

"Are you in the Union army?" President Davis asks the prisoner. "Or did you come down from Washington to see the show?"

"Aye," Congressman Ely says. "There were a bunch of us."

"That I can see," President Davis says. He looks far down the road that leads back to Washington. A mile away, the few thousand Yankee soldiers still able to fight are formed in a line of battle facing us. Behind them, hundreds of carriages carrying the various officials and civilian spectators dash down the road.

"I suppose your party didn't anticipate this development," President Davis says.

Congressman Ely nods and blushes, his face genuinely pathetic.

President Davis puts his arm around the congressman. "Well, Alfred, you're going to have to come back to Richmond with us, but I will make sure you are well attended."

He turns to the major. "Major, the congressman is yours."

The major takes Congressman Ely's arm and leads him away.

By now a crowd of a couple hundred soldiers has formed around us hoping to see President Davis. He raises his fist in the air and the soldiers erupt in cheers. I feel a tingle run across my skin as well.

"Gentlemen!" the president shouts. "The war is over. We have won the field. The day is ours."

Another burst of cheers goes out. Even I clap a little, because it really is cool to see in person this guy you've had to read about all your life. Dad would be going freaking nuts right now.

"Lead us on, sir! Let's chase 'em all the way to Washington!" cries Dupree.

"That hardly seems necessary," replies President Davis calmly as he turns to mount his horse.

Dupree grabs his shoulder.

"This is not the end but the beginning!" he rumbles. "We need to destroy them now!"

But his campaign voice isn't working on Davis.

"What's this?" President Davis snaps, swatting the hand away.

Under the glare of the president, Dupree falls to his knees

again, but quickly remembers himself and jumps back up.

"I'm sorry, sir!" Dupree sputters. He doesn't seem to know what to say. His face is flushed, eyes popping in rage. He doesn't look like the slick politician, but a raving lunatic struggling to keep his cool.

"I'm sorry, sir," he repeats, "but you are wrong. They will keep coming! We have won the field, you say? Unless we pursue them today, we will fight on this same soil a year from now. History books will call it the Battle of Second Manassas. And we will fight them at Fredericksburg, at Chancellorsville, in the Wilderness, and at Spotsylvania. We will try to bring the war to them at Sharpsburg and Gettysburg but we won't succeed and the war will come back to us. To Cold Harbor, to Petersburg, and finally to Appomattox. Along the way they will burn your crops, your barns and homes. They will destroy your cattle and steal your horses. They will confiscate your lands. They will throw you in a prison, sir, where you will stay for months before being released a bitter and broken man. And the rest of us will be left with nothing, sir. Nothing!"

Dupree is purple and spit flies from his mouth. Some of the soldiers seem moved by his speech, but Davis looks more annoyed than anything else.

"Yes, well," Davis begins, but Dupree interrupts.

"But I can change all that!" Dupree's hand shakes as he reaches into his pocket and pulls out a piece of paper. The map! Dupree's raving hasn't accomplished much, but the map could actually convince Davis. Then things could really get screwed up.

Telling the future to a couple of low-ranking officers is one thing. But the president of the Confederacy . . . now here's a man who could use that information. And with it win the war!

I take a step forward. Another. A few more steps and I can grab the map from Dupree. I don't know what I'll do next— maybe rip it up or eat it like spies do in the movies—but I've got to keep Davis from getting it.

Dupree is unfolding the map. My heart hammering inside my chest, I get ready to make a grab for it.

But I don't have to. Before I take a step, President Davis turns his back on Dupree and mounts his horse.

"I am afraid there's no time today, soldier, for me to peruse your documents," sniffs Davis. "Perhaps you could send them to my office in Richmond."

Dupree opens his mouth to speak, but President Davis turns his horse toward the bridge, jostling Dupree, who drops his precious map in the mud.

"It has been a long but prosperous day, my brothers," President Davis cries out. "Let us rejoice in it."

He gives his horse a kick with his heels and gallops back across the bridge. The soldiers cheer.

Shaking with fury, Dupree stoops down to pick up the map, which the horse has stomped into a shredded, muddy mess. As the other soldiers disperse, I nudge Cyrus and we move closer to Dupree. His eyes still follow President Davis, who grows smaller and smaller as the road winds away until he disappears over a hill.

"But I know what will come, Mr. President," we hear him saying. "And I can't rejoice."

* * *

The minutes pass. The Confederates around us grow fewer as they head back over the bridge. Even the ones Dupree had rallied are turning away now. Davis himself said they were done.

Dupree hasn't moved, but he's no longer trembling and his face has gone from red back to tan. Cyrus elbows me to follow him back to the others, but I'm not moving. Not until I know what Dupree is going to do.

I take my time picking up my musket and adjusting my gear so that I don't look too suspicious to Dupree. But he's not paying attention to me.

"He wouldn't even look at the map," mutters Dupree as he uses his sleeve to try to wipe off the mud. Suddenly he stops. He peers closer at the map, takes another swipe with the sleeve.

"Sherman," he gasps. "Sherman led the rearguard!"

Dupree jumps to his feet. From his pocket he fishes out a set of binoculars and looks through them.

Cyrus nudges me. "What are those? I ain't never seen . . ."

"It's him! Sherman!" Dupree hisses. "This time I'll take care of him myself!"

He drops the binoculars and picks up his rifle. He takes off through the cornfield toward the retreating Yankees, staying low so he won't be spotted.

Cyrus turns to me. "Well? Can we go now?"

"Not yet," I say. I grab Dupree's binoculars. Is it really *the* Sherman? The Yankee officers on horseback are about a quarter mile away. It's hard to tell from this distance, but one of them looks almost ugly enough to be Sherman. He's definitely got one of those jacked-up beards, but then again, they all do.

I turn to Cyrus.

"Come on!" I call. "We've got to stop him."

Cyrus crosses his arms and sniffs. "What for?" he asks. "Far as I can see, if the man wants to shoot a Yankee, let him do it. Not exactly fair play, but better one of them than one of us."

I want to scream, but there's no time. "Forget it," I say. "See you later."

Dupree is through the cornfield by the time I start running after him. But I can see he's already huffing and puffing from the run. His brain may tell him he's a soldier, but he's a reenactor in body. He's in even worse shape than my dad! He's only fifty yards away by the time I clear the corn.

Beyond him, on top of the hill, I see the Yankee officers turn and start to ride off toward the line of retreating Yankees. Dupree flops down on the ground and rests the barrel of his rifle on a rock to help him aim.

I look back, hoping that Cyrus has followed me. I really need him now, but he's nowhere in sight. It looks like it's up to me to stop Dupree.

I'm twenty yards away. My chest and legs burn as I scramble up the hill. Ten yards. I see Dupree pull back the hammer on his rifle. Sherman has one second to live.

"No!" I scream and throw myself on top of Dupree.

He rears up faster than I expect. He swings the rifle and the butt hits me in the chin. My head rings and all I can see are little dots of light as I tumble off of him.

143

"What the devil are you doing, boy?" he roars. "He got away! Do you know who that was?"

"Good," I wheeze through clenched teeth. It feels like my jaw is broken. He kicks me in the ribs. Hard. I can't seem to catch my breath.

"What did you say, boy? You ought to be ashamed to wear that uniform."

I can see again. I can see the tip of his bayonet pushing into the fabric of my jacket—pushing into my ribs. I can see pure hatred on his face. He pricks me again with the bayonet.

"What's this?" I hear him hiss.

I look down. His bayonet has pulled up my uniform to reveal a faded blue T-shirt underneath.

"What the—" gasps Dupree. He kneels down and yanks up the uniform to get a look at my shirt: "Are we having fun yet?"

"No," I groan. "Frankly, I'm having a sucky day and right now someone's shoving a bayonet in my stomach!"

"Who *are* you?" he roars.

"I'm from the future too. I'm not a real soldier, just a reenactor. Just like you. You don't have to kill me."

Now his face is inches from mine. Sweat drips from his nose.

"But maybe I will," he says. "You have no idea what I've done to get here." He gives a little smile and pushes the bayonet in a little farther. Now I can feel the metal on my skin. It's more pressure than pain, but I can't breathe too deep or the point pricks my ribs.

"I came here to set things right, boy," he whispers. "What about you?"

I snatch a quick breath. "No—I mean, yes!"

"You know who's up on that hill?"

I nod.

"You know what he's going to do? He's going to burn the whole Southland!"

I nod again.

"Davis was an idiot for letting them go. He doesn't know what's going to happen. But we do. Don't we, boy? Victory for the North. Reconstruction. The loss of our heritage. C'mon, we can go save it!"

"But—" I gasp.

"Listen, boy," he says, and his face is almost purple. There's spit at the corners of his mouth and tears stream from his eyes. "Right here, right now, we *are* somebody! We have status! Authority! My great-grandfather is a state senator, for Christ's sake! He has a plantation not fifty miles from here and all of it—the land, the fortune, the *power* will one day be mine! Except he's going to lose it all by the end of this war. Our heritage gone. Leaving us whites as nothing more than slaves."

"But what about the real slaves? What about their freedom?"

Dupree spits into the dirt. "Look at all the trouble they've caused. Integration. Affirmative action. Michael Jackson. Hip-hop music, for God's sake. I got a chance to erase all that. To make the South strong again. Imagine what I—no, what we could do here today. We can change the history books. And that would change the world."

I don't say anything. I figure as long as he wants to talk, that's better than him impaling me.

"Say Sherman was to somehow die today and he never gets a chance to torch our land. Say we pick off a couple other big shots and they never get a chance to fight our boys. Say we take care of Lincoln too . . . the war is then ours, and the South is free."

His eyes are wide now like he's the one in a trance. But slowly they narrow, and a smile cracks his face. "Who knows," he says, "maybe a stray bullet also kills our fair President Davis. Then an aspiring politician full of ideas for the future could come along . . . why, he could end up president of the Confederacy. I . . . I mean, he . . . could do it right."

His voice is a whisper now and he leans closer to me. "Think of all the battles that won't be fought. Think of all the men—from North and South alike—who don't need to die. The wives who will know their husbands, the children who will know their fathers. A few simple actions today will bring peace to this land. You can help me end this war."

After seeing a real battle today, seeing men die all around me, peace sounds pretty good. It's hard to argue with peace. But, I tell myself, it won't be peace for everybody.

"But you could end up making it all worse," I say. "You don't know—"

I gasp as the bayonet jabs deeper. I feel my shirt get clammy from my blood. "I'll take that chance," Dupree snarls. He glances over his shoulder at the retreating Yankees. "Sherman's halfway back to Washington. I've wasted too much time on you, boy. If you aren't going to help me, I can't have you around to hurt me. Are you with me? Last chance?"

You know how it is when somebody makes you so mad that your brain shuts off and you try to do something brave and fearless and Bruce Willis–like but you actually just do something stupid?

I grab the bayonet and shove upward with everything I've got. It does catch him by surprise and he does stagger backward and I do have a chance to jump to my feet. But, duh, the bayonet slashes through my hands like a Ginsu knife. I see blood all over his bayonet, and my palms are just gushing. My right hand got it a lot worse somehow. I clamp them both together real tight, but that doesn't help at all and just makes it hurt worse.

I was going to say something like "No way, buttmunch," but all I can do is squeak. So much for Bruce Willis.

"So I guess that was your answer, boy." He moves in closer, with the bayonet pointing right in my face. And just above the bayonet, the gun's muzzle looks as big as a cannon. Farther up the barrel, I see his index finger wrapping around the trigger like a snake and starting to squeeze.

I close my eyes, brace for the shot. Suddenly out of nowhere comes a sound—*ffffffft!* Dupree screams and drops the rifle. I open my eyes. Dupree is on his knees, a knife embedded in his neck. Blood pulses down the blade.

I whirl around to see where it came from. And there is Cyrus, his other Joshua knife in his hand, his arm cocked and ready to throw again.

"Thus always to tyrants," Cyrus says.

Shoot. That's the Bruce Willis line I was looking for.

Dupree grabs the knife's hilt and pulls the blade from his neck. Blood spurts out. Man, I thought my hands were gross. This is worse.

I stumble toward Cyrus.

"Cyrus, Cyrus, how—"

"Get down!" he yells. He jumps, grabs me, and we fall to the ground.

Dupree's musket explodes behind us. But I don't feel anything. I jump back to my feet.

But Cyrus doesn't get up. He doesn't move at all. He just lies there, facedown in the grass.

I reach down to grab him under the arm and help him up. This makes my hand go berserk with pain, but I only notice that for a second because that's when I see it. His pants and shirttail begin to turn a blackish red. Blood oozes up his white shirt.

Oh my God! He finally got that shot in the butt . . . while trying to save me.

I look up at Dupree. He's bleeding badly too. His left hand is clamped on his neck, trying to stop the blood. He falls over and lies still.

For a second we just all sit there bleeding. I'm having trouble thinking of what to do next. I'm going to have to do something about my hands, I know, because I'm getting dizzy and nauseous. But what exactly am I going to do?

"Stonewall!"

I look to the bridge and there is Ashby running to us. She runs straight toward me at first, but then she sees Dupree lying on the ground. She pauses and kneels down next to him. A couple of days ago, she probably would have panicked if she had seen her father with a wound like that. But after today, she knows what to do. She dumps out her nurse's bag and pulls several long strips from a big wad of vaguely clean linen.

"I've been so busy fighting him, I never even thought about him getting hurt," she says as she wraps up the knife wound on his neck. It's really messy. "I need to get him out of here."

For the first time she looks at me and at Cyrus.

She ties off her dad's bandage, checks out my hands, and starts wrapping them up. She looks over at Cyrus and grimaces.

"Did Dad do that? Jesus, I should just leave him here, but . . ."

"But you can't do that," I finish. "You can get his gun now. Take him back, I bet."

"You've got to come back too," she says.

I pull out the bugle. Yes, it's warm to the touch. Ready to go. This must be my time juncture. Time to get the heck out of here at last.

"But I can't leave Cyrus like this."

"Bring him too!" Ash says. "I mean, he'll die if you leave him here, so taking him to the future won't change history if that's what you're worried about. But we don't have time to worry about that now anyway. We gotta get them to a hospital." As she's saying this, she goes back over to her father to get the little silver gun. The Weapon. The Tempest Device that will take her and her father back.

I look down at the bugle. The Instrument. Can it really get me out of here and save Cyrus?

No, I remember, it can't.

I pull out Tom's letter and the instructions. It feels like a month since I looked at them, but it was only this morning. And, yes, I did remember correctly:

> The Instrument, the weakest of the Tempests, and the Weapon will be useful in traveling to the past, but note that they cannot take one into his own future nor can they be used to bring someone forward from the past since that person would be traveling into their own future though it be only the user's present . . .

The bugle and the gun can take me and Ash and Dupree back to our own proper times, but we'll vanish and Cyrus will be stuck here. Because those Tempests can't take him into his future. I can't decide if somebody made up these rules just to be a pain in my ass or if there's some real reason why people shouldn't go into the future.

Whatever. Like Ash said, there's no time to worry about this now. And there's no time to explain it all to her and to convince her to go without me.

"Yep, it looks like it's got one bullet left," she says, messing with the gun. "You ready?"

"Yes," I say, and I put the bugle to my lips.

But she grabs my arm for the second time today and pulls the bugle away. She leans forward and gives me a kiss—real quick, but a real kiss. Right on the lips.

"We did it, Stonewall," she says, almost smiling. "I'll see you in a second."

She puts her left hand on her father's shoulder and with the right she points the gun in the air.

"I hope this works," she says, and squeezes the trigger.

CHAPTER THIRTEEN

"**I HOPE** it works too," I say, dropping the bugle and turning back to Cyrus.

My mouth feels like it's on fire as I look at the spot where she and Dupree were just a second ago. My first kiss and I can't even savor it. I've got Cyrus to deal with.

Ash said he was going to die if he stayed here. Well, that's what was supposed to happen, I guess, in a footnote in a history book. But I don't care anymore about how things were *supposed* to be.

These Tempests are tools to let us change history, right? But the truth is that I've been running around all day nearly getting killed just to unchange history. That's good when it means keeping the South from winning the Civil War, but it stinks when it means killing Cyrus.

In the real history—before either me or Dupree did anything—Cyrus was supposed to get shot and die. But when we came back we changed the flow of the battle and Cyrus didn't die. Maybe it was when Dupree sent Cyrus charging for those

Parrott guns. Or maybe it was when Cyrus saved me from that Yankee lunatic at the start of the battle. Or maybe it was something even smaller that just moved Cyrus an inch or two out of the way of the fatal bullet.

Whatever it was, Cyrus somehow was saved. He made it through that whole battle without getting shot in his backside.

And if I hadn't been running around trying to stop Dupree, Cyrus would be back there with his buddies smoking his pipe, celebrating victory, and yakking away in his crazy Shakespeare-talk.

Really, I wouldn't be here if Dupree wasn't here. So in a crazy way Dupree saved Cyrus even though Dupree was the one who pulled the trigger, and I was the one who got Cyrus killed. Without even meaning to, I made history turn out the way it was supposed to turn out—and Cyrus has to pay for that by a painful death from his infected wound.

That's how it's supposed to be.

Well, the way things are supposed to be sucks.

Cyrus was *supposed* to get shot in the butt and lay here a couple of hours, maybe, until someone finds him and brings him to some pathetic makeshift hospital. There he was going to be put in front of a doctor who has probably never treated a bullet wound before today. But today he's already treated a couple of hundred. The doctor won't know about bacteria or germs or all the other crap that can happen to you. He will simply wash off a scalpel in a bucket of water already contaminated with the blood of a dozen other soldiers. His hands are also bloodied from these other soldiers as he cuts a hole and digs around in the wound to remove the bullet. The doctor won't know to give medicine or antibiotics to Cyrus. Antibiotics won't be invented for sixty more years. All he'll do is wrap some nasty rags around Cyrus's wounds and send him on his way.

Any wonder Cyrus's wound gets infected and he dies?

All right, that's it. I've made a decision. I'm going to do something—something that's not supposed to happen. Something that's going to at least make things better for Cyrus.

I'm just not sure what.

Man, I've watched enough movies, I should be able to do something.

I pick up some of the linen strips that Ash dumped out. At least maybe I can wrap up Cyrus's wound.

But as soon as I put them over the wound, Cyrus suddenly gasps, tries to sit up, and collapses again.

"Oh God!" he cries out and tries to grab his backside. I grab his arm to stop him from sticking his hand in the wound.

"Stonewall, you didn't run off this time, huh?"

"No, I—"

"Could you shut up for a second and do something! I think my ass is on fire."

"It's a bullet, Cyrus. Dupree, that crazy guy, shot you."

"Where is he, I'd like a chance to throw my other knife at him," says Cyrus, and for a second I see that crazy grin of his.

The grin is gone in a flash as another wave of pain shoots through his body.

"My flask!" he gasps. "Give it to me!"

"Hold on a second, this could be tricky," I say. The bullet hole is just under his back pocket, not an inch from his bottle of whiskey, or whatever it is. Shoot, in a movie the bullet would have hit the flask and Cyrus would be okay. But the flask is fine.

I try to ease it out of his pocket gently, but it still makes him wince. I try to roll him over a bit and my hand touches what feels like a pebble on his side.

"Ouch!" Cyrus hollers. "Give me that flask!"

He reaches for it, but I don't let it go. Instead, I touch the pebble again, and again he screams. "What in blazes are you doing?"

It's the bullet. It has traveled through his thigh and is lodged just under the skin.

This is the way it's supposed to happen.

"Stonewall, please. I need something to dull the pain."

Don't change the past. Don't change history.

"Please, Stonewall," he says.

But this is more than just history. This is Cyrus.

I take a deep breath. "Okay."

I uncork the bottle, but instead of giving it to him, I hold it to his lips to give him a small sip.

"More," he says. "More."

I ignore him and grab the knife that he was going to throw at Dupree. I pour a little of the alcohol on the blade.

"What are you *doing*?" he shouts. "The knife ain't hurt!"

"I'm sterilizing the blade," I say.

"*Steri*—what?"

"Don't worry about it," I tell him. "Just get ready."

I slit open his pants and there, almost like a pimple, is the end of the bullet just under the skin.

155

"No, sir," Cyrus says. "No, no, sir."

I undo the knot of my authentic reenactor's rope belt and shove it into Cyrus's mouth. "Bite down," I say. "Hard."

His jaw clenches. Before he can say anything else, I put the knife to the lump and cut.

"Aaargh!" Cyrus screams through the rope.

Cyrus's skin splits apart, revealing the lumpy lead bullet. With the tip of the knife, I quickly flick the thing out of Cyrus's thigh. The wound starts to gush.

Cyrus yanks the rope from his mouth. "Now give me that durn drink!"

I uncork the bottle and begin to pour the rest of it over the wound. The alcohol burns, and Cyrus lets me know it with a string of obscenities. I didn't know some of those words had been invented yet.

I give him a shove and roll him onto his stomach so I can pour the rest of the bottle on his butt shot. More screams and cussing, but I don't care. He doesn't understand that by digging out the bullet and pouring whiskey on his wound, I may have just saved his life. At least, I'm pretty sure that's what I saw on the History Channel once.

Cyrus is starting to go faint, his face pale and eyes droopy. I've got to plug up the wound, but I've used up all the rags Ash left.

That's when I remember the neckerchief. That stupid, super-nerd, Boy Scout reject neckerchief that my parents made me wear, which, by the way, I haven't seen ANYBODY else wearing today in the real war.

I ball it up, pour the rest of the whiskey on it, and stuff it in.

This is way too much for Cyrus. He screams again.

I remember my gym teacher's favorite bit of advice. I think it might actually work here.

"C'mon," I say, "walk it off."

It's a struggle, but I get him up. He leans on me while I wrap strips around his butt as best as I can.

We start moving. Man, it's going to be a long walk.

Cyrus gasps and groans with each step. We stagger back toward the stone bridge. I need to get him to the field hospital. I've done as much as I can, but how are we going to make it that far? I'm not sure I can go that far by myself, much less dragging Cyrus. But I can't leave him.

We're almost to the bridge when a figure suddenly appears from the shadows beneath it and runs toward a low rock wall to the north. The figure is crouched so low to the ground that I barely notice it. It disappears behind the wall for a second, then jumps over the wall and starts running across the field toward the retreating Yankees.

"Jacob!" I cry out.

He whirls around with a look of surprise.

"It's me, Jacob," I call. "Please help us."

He seems to stand frozen forever. As if he's stuck in the mud and can't get out.

"Jacob, please," I call again, as Cyrus's body starts to crumple to the ground. "I can't hold him anymore."

Still he doesn't move. What is he doing? I need help!

Jacob glances toward the Union army and back again at the stone bridge. Now I see what he's doing. He's not just some kid running across a bridge and through a field. He's a slave trying to escape. Trying to make it to the Yankees. To his liberators. To freedom.

"Forget it! I'm sorry!" I yell quickly. "Just go! Go! Go!"

But it's too late. A unit of Confederates—new arrivals who haven't seen a bit of action yet—begins to cross the stone bridge. There must be two hundred of them in a long column.

Jacob runs toward us and slips his head under Cyrus's other arm.

"I'm sorry, Jacob," I say. "I'm so sorry. I didn't realize . . ."

I look at Jacob, but his face is blank and cold. He could have been halfway to the Union army by now. He could have had a new life and I ruined it.

"I'm really sorry," I say again, but by now we're at the bridge. The column of troops parts, and together, Jacob and I bear Cyrus across Bull Run and head for the hospital.

"Hang on, Cyrus. I can see the stretchers now. We're almost there."

Up ahead is Wilmer McLean's barn. The wounded lie in rows on the ground beside it, waiting their turn for the surgeons inside.

Cyrus blacked out just after we crossed the bridge and has been dead weight for most of the mile we've trudged. But I haven't stopped talking to him the whole way, if anything just to keep me going. Jacob hasn't said a word, not even when we passed Mr. Robinson's house a little ways off to our right and up a hill. I saw the old man standing on his front porch with his hands on his hips and I waved as best I could without letting Cyrus fall. But he didn't wave back. He just watched us walk past.

I told Jacob he should go, but he didn't even glance at the old man.

Still, despite my bayonet wound—and how many guys at my school could claim that?—and the fact that my legs and chest burn from carrying Cyrus, for the first time today I feel kind of relieved. Cyrus has his butt shot, but I'm hopeful I saved his life, and that I haven't caused too many problems for the future.

Sure, we'll have to deal with Dupree back in the present, but at least his chance of mucking up history is over. Mission accomplished. My work here is done. I've still got to figure out something to do for Jacob, but all in all, I feel pretty good.

Until we stagger into the field hospital.

Bloodied soldiers lie all around us. Loud screams come from inside the barn. Stacked up outside the barn door is a small pile of amputated legs and arms. A man drenched in blood emerges from the barn's dark interior bearing another bloody leg while two others, who are hoisting a stretcher with a wounded soldier, pass him on their way to the surgeons inside.

Jacob and I lay Cyrus on his stomach on the ground in line with the other wounded. His pants and the back of his shirt are soaked with blood. I turn his head to the side to make sure he can breathe. Now all I can do is wait. I've done all I can for Cyrus. My head spins and I collapse to my knees and puke until there's nothing left to come out.

An orderly comes up and holds a canteen to Cyrus's mouth. The orderly pulls down Cyrus's pants a bit to inspect the wound.

"The bullet's already out," I say.

"That's good," the orderly says. "He'll be all right." He looks up at me. "Is he your kin?"

"He sure is," I say.

The orderly nods to Jacob, who hasn't moved or said a word since being relieved of his burden. "Is he yours?"

Of course we're not related, I almost say, until I realize what he meant. "Oh, no. He's nobody's. I think he's free now."

The orderly makes a nasty sound. I guess it's a laugh, but it's an ugly one. "Well, he ain't free no more," he says, clamping his hand on Jacob's arm. "We got plenty for him to do. Let's go, boy."

"Wait!" I cry. The orderly looks curiously at me. I should have said Jacob did belong to me and then later tonight try to help him escape. I've got to do something. But all I can think of to say is, "His name's Jacob."

The orderly looks at me even more strangely. "So?"

He begins walking off with Jacob in tow. I want Jacob to at least turn around so I can say good-bye.

"I couldn't have done it without you, Jacob," I call after him. "I'm glad you were here."

But Jacob doesn't even turn around. The orderly yanks his arm and they disappear into the shadows of the barn.

I sit at Cyrus's side the rest of the afternoon, waiting for his turn in the barn. The orderly left a canteen for us and every few minutes I hold it to Cyrus's lips and let some water trickle out.

From time to time, Jacob reappears from the barn carrying amputated limbs or toting in another wounded soldier. I see him out of the corner of my eye, but he doesn't look at me and I don't look too long at him. I managed to prevent him from doing the one thing he really wanted to do—escape. But hopefully what we did today will help lead to his freedom in a few years.

I try explaining all of this to Cyrus as we wait, but he's still passed out. After I say everything there is to say about Jacob, I tell Cyrus stories about the craziness of my father and his reenacting friends. How they spend most of their weekends traveling to Civil War battlefields and wearing old, scratchy clothes and sleeping on the ground. I tell him how half of the reenactors are so out of shape that they must stop after a few minutes of marching to catch their breath and eat a snack. I tell him about how the reenactors aim their muskets above the heads of the "enemy."

And I tell him that if they could see what I've seen today, and what I'm seeing all around me right now, they would never dream of spending their weekends reenacting it.

The sun is setting behind the hills and a gray duskiness settles along the green fields. The smell of tobacco fills the air and campfires spark all around me as soldiers start boiling their coffee.

Finally, two orderlies appear with a stretcher and place it beside Cyrus. I'm glad Jacob isn't one of them. As they lift Cyrus onto it, I realize I won't see him again. It is time for me to go back and I want to say good-bye. But he is still out of it.

I think about writing a quick note, saying I am proud to be his great-great-great-great-nephew, but he'll just think I'm crazy. I reach into my pockets for something to leave with him and feel the five packets of McLean's tobacco I'd bought for him. I slip them into his pockets and pat his back.

"I hope this makes us even," I say. And the orderlies carry him away.

I stand up, gaze around the field one more time, and unsling the bugle from my shoulder. Darkness is falling and the campfires sparkle like stars across the fields. I hold the bugle to my lips and feel relief that the cool metal quickly blazes with heat.

Without even thinking about what to play, I begin to blow the slow, mournful tune of taps.

CHAPTER FOURTEEN

"UH, TOM? Here's your bugle back."

I'm standing at the entrance of Tom's Emporium on Sutler's Row. It's dark now and the stars are out. Inside the tent, a lantern glows. Tom's face flickers in the orange light. He puffs on a pipe. The tobacco smells sweet—too sweet for me. Exhaustion hits me, my head reels, and I start to faint.

In a flash, Tom is at my side. "Whoa, son," I hear him say. He catches me with his good arm and helps me into his tent. He sits me down on his folding chair. Its coolness revives me. I open my eyes. Tom gives me a nice smile, a sympathetic smile.

He takes the bugle from my fingers.

"I'm sorry I had to do that to you, Hinkleman, but I'm too old to go back and so are most of these reenactors. I needed somebody smart, somebody who might pass for a regular soldier, and somebody who knew the stakes."

It takes a second for this to sink in.

"So you knew what the bugle would do?" Now I'm not

feeling faint. I'm feeling mad. "Why didn't you tell me? I could have been killed! I could have . . ."

"I know," says Tom. He actually looks a little ashamed as he stares down at the bugle. In the lantern light, I see that the bugle has lost its shine. Once again, it's just a dirty, dented horn. "I'm sorry. But you seemed like a smart kid who could keep out of trouble."

I pull my T-shirt up to show him the gash on my chest from Dupree's bayonet. I hold out my hands so he can see the bloody bandages over my palms. "It's not so easy keeping out of trouble in the middle of a freaking CIVIL WAR!" I yell at him. "I'm lucky I'm not dead."

Tom puts down the bugle, reaches back into the old trunk, and takes out a small plastic box with a big red cross on it. A first aid kit.

Even with just one arm, he easily unwraps my nasty bandages and pops open the kit.

"Do you know what you're doing?" I ask, still ticked off.

He tears open an alcohol swab with his teeth. "One thing I do know about is wounds," he says. "Hold on, this'll hurt."

The alcohol burns like crazy. And this is just for a couple of scrapes on my hand. Now I know why Cyrus passed out. But Tom doesn't seem to notice. In just a few seconds, I've got antibiotic ointment and sterile bandages over my cuts.

"Probably could have used some stitches earlier," he says, "but too late now. You'll have some nice scars."

He looks up at my face. "And it looks like you got off better than Dupree. Ambulance showed up a couple of hours ago and took him away."

I can't help but grin a little. "Yeah, Cyrus did that!"

"Who?" Tom asks.

I picture Cyrus being carried into the barn, and just as quick my smile fades away.

"My kin," I tell Tom.

Tom pats my leg. "You'd better start from the beginning. Tell me everything that happened, especially everything that involves Dupree."

Tom listens to my story. I tell him everything—about Cyrus and Big Jim and Elmer. About everything Dupree did and didn't do, and everything he wanted to do. I tell him about how I came across an unexpected ally in Ashby.

"So that's who was with Dupree in the ambulance," Tom interrupts. He strokes his beard. "Yes, that makes sense now. Ashby . . . as in Turner Ashby—very possibly the craziest officer I ever ran into. But don't you see, Stonewall? Too many people think this war was just something that happened in the past. But it's not just the past. It is our present too, and our future. It marks all of us today as clearly as you two are marked by your names—Stonewall and Ashby."

He gives me a wink. "And you certainly could have found a worse-looking ally."

I'm glad it's dark in the tent, because I feel my face blush. I go on with my story, about the captured cannons and Mrs. Henry and Mr. Robinson and Jacob. I mention General Bee and notice that Tom tears up. He completely believes the whole story. I know every other person alive would think I'm crazy, but he's actually smiling when I finish.

"Well done, young Stonewall. I knew you could do it. I knew you'd be smart enough to stop him."

"But don't you think I messed things up? I mean, I wasn't supposed to be there. I could have changed history!" Jacob comes into my mind. I bow my head and whisper, "I did change history."

Tom looks genuinely upset. "You mean Jacob?"

I nod.

Tom is silent for a moment.

"This is war, Stonewall. And there's always sacrifice in war. Perhaps you did change history. Perhaps for the better. Perhaps for the worse. I remember that after the battle several slaves were shot while trying to escape. Maybe one was your Jacob. Maybe you saved his life."

I shake my head. "I've never read anything about that before."

Tom shrugs. "It's not in any books. I've just got a pretty good memory."

I try to take comfort in this. Maybe the Confederates on the stone bridge would have shot Jacob as he ran toward the Yankees. It's tough to say. Tough all around.

"Believe me, Stonewall, all people—be they from my century or your century or the century of Jesus Christ himself—have at least one regret for something they've done in the past. I know I do. After seeing all I've seen, what this country has become and what it *could* have become had the war turned out differently—Dupree's way, if you will—I regret I took up arms against the country I had sworn before God to defend.

But I'm lucky too. With your help, I actually have a chance to redeem myself. And my country."

"There are things in the present worth fighting for in the past," I say.

Tom nods. "You at least understood that much."

He takes a lemon from his pocket, holds it in his mouth, and with his good hand flicks open a knife and cuts the fruit in two. He offers me half and this time I take it. The sourness floods my mouth.

"But why didn't you tell me?"

"Would you have believed?"

"Good point," I agree. "But why me?"

Tom spits out some pulp and tosses the rind to the ground. He looks at me, cocks his head, and gives me another wink.

"Let's just say I recognized you."

"But I've never seen you at another reenactment."

"You're right about that," Tom says with a grin. "It wasn't at a reenactment. It was somewhere a bit more . . . ah, authentic, shall we say."

It takes a second, but when it hits me I almost gag on the lemon. "You mean from the war! From the battle! You remember me from the real battle!"

He holds the smile for a second, but it fades and his eyes go hazy. He opens his mouth but doesn't speak. Finally he whispers, "I told you I had a pretty good memory."

I feel my face go hot again. "I made such a fool of myself."

Just as quick his blue eyes light up. "Don't you ever say that again! You did good. Real good. As good as any man I ever commanded."

We stand in silence for a moment.

"Thanks, Tom," I say. "I mean, uh, Stonewall."

Now Tom looks down. "I'd rather you call me Tom," he says. "I've always hated the name Stonewall."

Ditto that.

"So the question is, my young conscript . . ." Tom says.

"So I'm still a conscript?"

He holds out the bugle.

"Not anymore. You're a soldier now. The question is, will you fight again if our country calls?"

The morning is bright and warm as my parents and I pile into the car to ride home. I immediately lay my head against the back window and close my eyes. But I still can't go to sleep.

I couldn't sleep at all last night after coming back, even though the moonshine-drinking yahoos at the next campsite were passed out before midnight. Events from the day kept playing in my mind. Finally, I grabbed a flashlight and spent the rest of the night retracing my journey through the Battle of Bull Run. Here is where I met Cyrus. Here is Mrs. Henry's house. Here are replicas of the Union cannons we captured. Here is the foundation of Mr. Robinson's house. Here is the stone bridge.

At least now I don't have to ask my father where Uncle Cyrus got shot. Last night, I stood where it happened, and wondered if Cyrus survived.

I wonder that still.

Trying not to sound too sarcastic or strange, I ask Dad, "What happened to our uncle Cyrus after Bull Run?"

He looks at me through the rearview mirror with this curious expression on his face. It's like he's waiting for a wisecrack, so I try to stare back as innocently as I can—something I don't have much practice at.

"Like we've told you a dozen times before, he's cited for bravery in the Official Records by none other than your namesake, Stonewall Jackson himself!"

"Right," I say. "For the Battle of Bull Run."

"Bull Run?" Dad says. "You sure you're feeling all right? You mean the Battle of Antietam?"

Antietam! That was in 1862 . . . a year after Bull Run!

"Yes, sir," Dad says. As if reading aloud, he says, "'Sergeant Hinkleman assumed command of the company and staunched the enemy's advance until the arrival of reinforcements . . .'"

He survived! He lived! And sergeant too! He was only a private at Bull Run! This is great! He—

"'. . . when he at last succumbed to his injuries and perished.'"

My head swims and my gut feels like it's been hit. Hard. "Perished?"

Dad gives me another strange look. "Stonewall, you okay?"

"Yes," I say, trying to keep my eyes from tearing up. "I'd just have liked to have known him."

My parents glance at each other. Just as quickly they turn back to the road, like looking too long may break whatever

169

spell I'm apparently under. But the grin on my father's face lets me know they are proud of me.

We drive in silence for a while, and slowly my sadness becomes something else. Something like contentment. Thanks to me, Cyrus lived one more year and got to die a hero at Antietam. Beats a legacy of simply being shot in the butt.

I think about telling my parents what happened. But they might not be proud of that. They would probably make me go see that counselor again. And up my Ritalin prescription.

"Stonewall, I really appreciate your change in attitude," my dad says a few minutes later. "I tell you what. Your mom and I have been talking. You're old enough to stay by yourself. In September when we go to the Antietam reenactment, you don't have to come."

The Battle of Antietam. The bloodiest day of the Civil War. The bloodiest day in American history.

The day Cyrus dies.

I reach inside my pack and feel the cool metal of the bugle.

Stonewall's bugle.

"Oh, that's okay," I say. "I'll go."

LET'S TALK ABOUT IT!

THE BATTLE of Bull Run is just the first of many, many battles in the Civil War. The men who died that day were the first of more than half a million who died in the war. What do you think would have happened if Abraham Lincoln hadn't sent troops to the South to fight? What would America look like today if the South had been successful in seceding from the Union?

Is Cyrus a good guy? How about Big Jim? Or any of the Confederate soldiers? How does it make you feel to know these men fought a war to protect the idea that some people can be bought and sold and used as slaves? What does that say about them as human beings?

Time travel is a popular subject for books and movies. But could it really work? Many paradoxes have been suggested, such as the tree paradox. Say you carve your initials in a tree at suppertime. Then you go back in time to lunchtime and cut the tree down. What will happen at suppertime? Will you still be able to carve your initials in it?

Stonewall has a long list of things he misses while re-enacting, such as video games and soda. What would you miss most if you have to pretend to live in the 1860s for a weekend? Nothing with batteries. Nothing with plastic. And no junk food.

Ashby is probably a lot tougher and braver than Stonewall when you get down to it. But it's hard for her to do anything because of the limited role that women played in the battles. Why do you think women were made to stay away from the battlefield, and what was their role during the Civil War?

Stonewall has a lot of bad things to say about re-enactors, most of which is just because he is a big whiner. But he does raise an interesting point. Is it right to re-enact a war? Is it wrong to make a hobby out of what was a very real horror? Or is this a great way to bring history to life and honor the actions of the soldiers?

When an officer yelled "Charge!", soldiers were expected to do it. Imagine that you are a part of a line of men. Across a field from you are more men, armed with weapons. You have no armor and no shield. You know that many of the men in your line will die, and there's a good chance you might die, too. Would you charge? What types of things are you willing to fight for?

TEST YOUR KNOWLEDGE!

1. What is a sutler?

2. What happened to Mrs. Henry?

3. What is Tom's last name?

4. Who gives Stonewall Jackson his name?

5. Who was Jefferson Davis?

6. What did Dupree use to go back in time?

7. Who was Ashby named after?

8. What does "Farby" mean?

9. Who wrote the instructions for the Tempests?

10. Where did Cyrus come from?

DO YOU KNOW
ALL THE ANSWERS?

1. Who is Ashby named for, and what did she do?

2. Bull Run was the first real battle of the Civil War but not the first time shots were fired. When did the fighting really begin?

3. Why is the First Battle of Bull Run also called "First Manassas"?

4. Dupree really wanted to kill Sherman. Why? What's the big deal about Sherman?

5. The bullets some soldiers used were called minie balls, but they weren't shaped like balls. So how did they get that name?

6. Why did Tom have only one arm?

7. Were teenagers as young as Stonewall really allowed to participate in battles? See if you can find a picture of one online.

8.   Benjamin Franklin seems to have figured out the Tempests. Possibly they are connected to his experiments with electricity. In real life, what exactly was he doing with electricity? Did he actually discover anything?

9.   Was Stonewall Jackson a Yankee? Maybe so. Check out his hometown.

10.   If Dupree ends up going back in time to the Second Battle of Bull Run, which events could he change to affect the outcome of that battle? How could Stonewall stop him?